paper faces

Dot didn't want anything to change. She'd had enough of that. Change was unsettling. It meant brick dust and disorder. The war was over and she was afraid.

May, 1945. Dot ought to be happy, but she isn't. Everything is changing, she's being moved from one place to another, and nothing is the same any more. Dot has to learn to cope with death, illness, and the return of the father who is a stranger to her. She begins to discover that there are different ways of looking at historical events, different kinds of truth, and many ways of being afraid and being brave.

'Rachel Anderson has written what is in one sense an historical novel, in another a profound study of self-discovery, and by any standards a rich and deeply moving story of childhood . . . The book is masterly in its control of narrative, but the reader is aware not of technical excellence but of understanding and tender, tough humour. This is a very fine book indeed.'   *The Junior Bookshelf*

Paper Faces won the Guardian Children's Fiction Award in 1992.

RACHEL ANDERSON was born at Hampton Court during the war, and on 8 May 1945 watched her grandmother hanging paper Union Jacks on the laurel bushes around the front door. She and her husband have four children. She has worked in radio and newspaper journalism, and has written four books for adults, though now writes mostly for children. When not writing she is involved with the needs and care of children who are socially or mentally challenged.

D1341082

paper faces

OTHER BOOKS BY RACHEL ANDERSON

The Poacher's Son
The War Orphan
French Lessons
The Bus People
When Mum Went to Work
The Working Class
Black Water
The Doll's House

For young readers
Little Angel Comes to Stay
Little Angel, Bonjour
Happy Christmas, Little Angel

Oxford Myths and Legends
Renard the Fox

paper faces

Rachel Anderson

Oxford University Press

Oxford New York Toronto

Oxford University Press, Great Clarendon Street, Oxford OX2 6DP

Oxford New York
Athens Auckland Bangkok Bogota Bombay
Buenos Aires Calcutta Cape Town Dar es Salaam Delhi
Florence Hong Kong Istanbul Karachi
Kuala Lumpur Madras Madrid Melbourne
Mexico City Nairobi Paris Singapore
Taipei Tokyo Toronto

and associated companies in
Berlin Ibadan

Oxford is a trade mark of Oxford University Press

Copyright © Rachel Anderson 1991
First published 1991
First published in paperback 1997

A CIP catalogue record for this book is available
from the British Library

Cover design by Slatter-Anderson

ISBN 0 19 271614 X

Printed and bound in Great Britain by
Biddles Ltd, Guildford and King's Lynn

Contents

1 The Day the Peace Began

In the afternoon, the landlady hung a line of coloured bunting along the fence outside her house. Gloria and Dot rented a room in the basement. Gloria led Dot up the outside steps from the basement to look at the cotton flags flapping in the sun. Women from along the street came out of their front doors too.

Gloria gave Dot a hug and said, 'Take a peek at that, Dot. So you won't never forget today. Today's ever so special.' Then she took a little tin brooch from her pocket. It was in the same colours as the bunting, red, white and blue.

'There you are, ducks. That's a victory token, V for victory.'

Onè of the grown-ups from along the street noticed the brooch and said to Gloria, 'You're in luck! Where d'you find that? We went up Derry and Tom's yesterday. They was sold clean out. Not as much as a secondhand Union Jack left.'

'Got it for her week before. Last one they had in,' said Gloria, and she pinned the tin brooch on to Dot's cardigan. 'So you mind you keep it safe as houses, Dot, then you'll always remember.'

'Is it over then?' said Dot.

' 'Course it's over, you silly goose,' said Gloria.

'Over now,' Dot repeated, but she wasn't sure what it meant and if she even wanted it over. It sounded insecure.

One of the grown-ups said, 'I was hoping for a bit of a fly-past.' Another said, 'I'd a thought you'd had enough of that by now!'

They stood around hopefully, occasionally glancing up

1

into the sky or peering down the road as though expecting something to happen. When nothing did, they drifted indoors again.

So Gloria and Dot went back down the area steps to their room, leaving the sunshine behind. It was always dim down here but Gloria didn't switch the light on because of being told to save electricity. There was always a faint smell, too, of something rotting.

'Just the gas,' said Gloria. 'Escaping. It won't do us no harm.'

They hadn't had gas in their last room.

Gloria lay on the bed and thumbed through the pages of her magazine. *Picturegoer* was about film stars. Gloria liked reading about the stars. She knew all their names. Sometimes she tried to do her hair like some of them in the photographs.

Dot could hear the landlady listening to her radio next door in the kitchen.

After that, nothing happened for hours till Gloria suddenly said, 'Listen, ducky, I'm going to pop up the West End. Just see what's going on. Mrs Parvis'll keep an eye on you. Won't be back late, promise. All right, love?'

She took her best outfit from the paper carrier on the mantleshelf, shook it to get rid of the creases, and soon was all dressed up and ready to go with her red lipstick, her pretty pinned-up hair and her fancy black peep-toe shoes.

'You look nice,' said Dot. 'Like a real star.'

Gloria was pleased. She wanted to be like a star. She never wore slacks because she said stars didn't. She said they mostly wore silky slips and dressing-gowns.

Gloria tucked the blanket around Dot and kissed the tip of her nose.

Dot said, 'But what about Baby?'

They hadn't been to see him today. Would it matter?

'Not one day won't make no difference to him,' said Gloria. 'Today's ever so special. Maybe you don't understand. You will one day.'

Of course Dot understood. She'd heard the landlady say

how it was all over now bar the shouting. 'He'll be right as rain, pet,' said Gloria. 'And we'll be seeing him to-morrow.'

Dot tried not to mind being left on her own in the basement. With their two paper carriers on the shelf, the scrappet of carpet on the concrete floor, and the gas fire in the corner it was almost beginning to feel like home. The last place they were in they didn't even have a proper bed.

As she lay listening to the sound of the grown-ups' laughter coming through the wall, Dot felt round the sharp tin edges of her victory brooch still pinned to her cardigan front and remembered how Gloria had once said you'd always be safe in a place like this. 'Even if the whole house collapsed on top of you. They'd never get you down here.'

There was more noise than usual coming through from the landlady's kitchen. Then they began singing. Dot remembered how sometimes there used to be singing down in the shelters in the dark. But this singing was different, not quiet holy hymns but loud and impassioned. They must be having a party in there. Dot wished, after all, that Gloria hadn't gone out because Gloria liked parties and now she was missing it.

Dot was hungry. There hadn't been a proper tea. They hadn't been to visit Baby in hospital either. What a strange unsettling day. She knew she wouldn't forget it, even without her victory token.

Dot woke when she heard Gloria coming down the clanky metal steps outside, heard her stumble her way across the room, and then felt herself being pushed to the far side of the bed.

'Shove over there,' said Gloria. 'Make a bit of room. Age before beauty.'

When Gloria climbed in beside her, they both rolled down into the dip in the middle of the bed. Dot felt Gloria snuggling up close.

'You're nice and warm, pet,' Gloria said. 'Ooh, Dot, I do wish I'd took you. It was wonderful! You don't know the half of it. There was thousands of us!'

3

Dot put her arm round her mother's neck and hugged to show she was still awake and listening.

'We saw the King. And the Queen. And the princesses. We shouted for them till they came out on their balcony. Then we danced, right there in front of the palace. And we sang. And there was the searchlights up in the sky. And down King Edward's docks all them boats was letting off their hooters.'

Dot tried hard to imagine it. She said, 'I think they had a party here too. In Mrs Parvis's kitchen.'

'Did they? I'm glad of that. So you weren't lonely? I would've come back sooner. But all the roads were that crowded. I couldn't find a bus nowhere. Drivers must've been celebrating too. So I had to walk all the way.'

'Was it a long way?' Dot wondered.

'Not too far when you're having a good time. You know, pet, I been thinking. From now on everything's going to be all right. I just know it. Like they said. We've won ourselves a new world. Well, better get some shut-eye. Nighty-night, pet. God bless.'

When Dot heard the deep slow breathing of her mother sleeping, she was alone again and she was frightened. People had been saying that once the war was over, things would change. Dot didn't want anything to change. She'd had enough of that. Change was unsettling. It meant brick dust and disorder. The war was over and she was afraid.

2 Dot's Baby

The next day things were back to normal. Gloria tied on her red headscarf, Dot buttoned up her pink cardigan and they went to wait for the bus to take them down to the hospital to see how Baby was doing. The only difference from usual was the tin brooch. And they saw quite a lot more flags hanging out of windows.

It was always a long wait at the bus stop, followed by a long ride. Gloria said it wasn't half as bad as the last place. When he'd first been taken poorly, Baby had been driven in an ambulance from one hospital to another. They never seemed to be near where Gloria and Dot were. It was like cat and mouse trying to keep up with him.

'He's more like a little sparrow, ain't he?' said Gloria. 'Always hopping around, never stopping put in one spot.'

One time, the people at the hospital didn't even tell Gloria that Baby had been moved. When she and Dot turned up to visit, he just wasn't there any more.

'Oh, but he's been transferred,' said the nurse. 'You must have known.' She didn't seem at all bothered that Gloria and Dot would have to go trudging off to another hospital somewhere else to find him.

Gloria became angry. 'We come up all this way to visit. Now you tell me he ain't even here!'

The nurse just said, 'Well what d'you expect *me* to do about it? Burst into flames for you?'

The latest hospital was built tall, of blackish-red bricks, with rows of dark windows reaching upwards towards the sky.

'What d'you think it's like in a ward right up top?' Dot said. 'D'you think it's like flying? D'you think it's frightening?

5

They could get you more easy up there, couldn't they?'

'Don't drag. Keep up with me,' said Gloria. 'You're more bear than squirrel today. I don't want to go losing you in here.'

Dot knew there must be people up there in the vulnerable places on the top floor because on their way through the draughty corridors they passed the lift-shafts, each with its rattling metal cage and fearful loops of cable and black rope dangling beneath like greasy snakes. The lifts were for transporting patients too sick to protest to departments on higher floors.

Luckily, they didn't have to get into the cage for the children's ward was on the ground floor. Gloria went in. Dot stood outside the double swing doors. She wasn't allowed any further. Children couldn't go into the children's ward unless they themselves were poorly.

The corridor was dark brown. Gloria had said it was painted like that so it wouldn't show the blood. But when Dot said, 'What blood?' Gloria laughed and said, 'No, not really, pet. Just pulling your leg.'

The ground floor windows were barred like a prison, so nobody could climb in or out. And they were glazed with opaque white glass so that the patients couldn't see out either, nor passers-by see in. Dot hoped it was nice for Baby in there.

Visiting him the day after the peace began, everything was the same as always. Dot waited and waited in the long brown corridor with nowhere to sit. Once some nurses bustled along. Then an empty bed was wheeled by.

When it was time to go home again, at the hospital gates the friendly porter was on duty, sitting inside the cosy little wooden porters' hut. It would have made a compact little home except it was painted dark brown like the corridors. The porter recognized Gloria and leaned out of his hut.

'Hello there, dear. And how's the little laddie doing today?'

Gloria half nodded her head and shrugged. 'No change,'

she said, giving an elusive and empty smile. 'Not so you'd notice.'

Dot was glad. She felt safe. Changes were always bad. No change must be good. The nearly worst thing that could happen would be her father coming back. It had to happen one day, but not yet. And the very worst thing would be having to move again. But she didn't tell Gloria.

They were back at Mrs Parvis's just in time for the evening meal. 'By the skin of our teeth!' said Gloria as they scurried for their places at table. It was called High Tea. Here too, there were still no changes that Dot could see. Always toast and dripping followed by a good hot dish. Today's main dish was cabbage and swede stew with dumplings. Dot liked the reassuring look of those dumplings, plump and pale, floating amongst the shreds of yellowish green in the huge pan.

'Now that it's over, you'd expect they'd start getting things right at last, wouldn't you?' said Mrs Parvis, standing up at the end of the table to ladle out to her assembled household.

'Well, things are bound to start looking up soon,' said one of the lodgers. 'I mean, they *promised*, didn't they?'

'I'm glad it's finished. But I still got that feeling that we *lost* something. Know what I mean?'

Dot listened as the grown-ups continued to grumble along as they had done for as long as she could remember, like the harmless rumble of gunfire faraway.

'For myself,' Mrs Parvis went on, 'I'd have felt more excited like, if it'd finished *last* summer. When we all thought it would. Somehow I can't feel so interested in the peace now. I feel sort of, "So what?" Don't you agree, Mr Brown?'

Mr Brown gazed down at his plate and nodded. Mrs Parvis always made him agree with whatever she said. Gloria said he only went along with her because of the housing shortages, because he knew he was lucky to have a room at all, even if it was only half a room at Mrs Parvis's.

Mr Brown's room, first landing, back, was tall and

7

narrow like a thin passage. It was a sliver of a larger room that had been partitioned off. Dot peeked in when he was out at work. She wanted to see what there was out of that lanky half-window. Downstairs in the basement, all they had to look at was the brick wall of the coal-hole with Mrs Parvis's aluminium meat-safe hanging on it, and a line of smelly bins. Mr Brown's half-room turned out to be nearly as dark as the basement because of the cardboard panes stuck in the window where the glass had been blown out. That was ages ago. They'd still not been replaced.

Dot didn't hear Mrs Parvis come creeping up behind her.

'Prying! I've warned you before, you young hoyden,' Mrs Parvis scolded. 'I will not tolerate children wandering around wherever their fancy takes them! Whatever will Mr Brown think!'

Dot knew that Mrs Parvis couldn't care less what Mr Brown thought because Mr Brown didn't count for anything, because poor Mr Brown had never been in uniform. Dot had heard Mrs Parvis say that it was a crying shame, a young fit man like that. He was a steel-cutter in the aircraft factory. He was missing two fingers from his right hand. They would never grow again. Dot didn't like watching that two-fingered hand as it grasped the knife to cut the dumplings. Mr Brown did not like to show it either. At High Tea, Dot was glad when he saw her staring and tidied the strange hand out of sight beneath the table. Using only his whole hand, he had to dissect his dumpling with the edge of the fork.

Cutting steel to make aeroplane bodies was a dangerous job.

'There's over a million homeless in London,' Mrs Parvis grumbled on. 'It's gonna take years to put that right.'

'If you'll pardon the correction, not so much as a million,' said one of the lady lodgers. 'I saw the official figures released last week by the Ministry of Information. A hundred and thirty thousand London homes destroyed, so the precise number of homeless is now estimated to be around only a quarter of a million.'

Mrs Parvis ignored the interruption and carried on. 'Single men won't come top of the list for rehousing, not by a long chalk.' She eyed Mr Brown meaningfully over her hot cauldron of cabbage before going on with her set piece. 'First they let us have this great feeling of elation. It's over, we thought. But that only lasted a week or two, didn't it? Now it's like they're saying the party's finished. It seems to me, everything's going on just the same as it was before. Except there's less of this and less of that. Which is why I'll be obliged if you don't ask for bread unless you really want it. I queued a long time for that loaf. And I've no doubt it's the last we'll be seeing till Thursday.'

Dot waited for her share of the hot dish. She was served last. Mrs Parvis gave her a reduced portion. Dot watched half a dumpling sliding on to her plate. As Mrs Parvis had explained to Gloria when they first arrived, 'I'm in no position to go showing no favouritisms to some and not to others. If you ask me, that's the first step to black market. What if everybody was demanding full portions for their children? There's been people starved to death in Stalingrad, so don't you go thinking you're something special.'

While Gloria helped dry the dishes after tea, Mrs Parvis continued to find fault with the people who ran the country.

'They'll nag us now about winning the *peace*, just like they nagged us about winning the *war*. And I don't suppose my old man'll be home for months. Heard from your hubby? Does he know about the poor little kiddy?'

Gloria shrugged.

'R.A.F. isn't it? Not expected back for quite a while yet, I suppose? Something very hush-hush, didn't you say?'

Dot knew that her father was at a place that Gloria rarely talked to other people about, but kept like some kind of secret. Some days, Dot couldn't remember what his face was like. She looked at the snapshot of him in Gloria's handbag, but still couldn't seem to see him properly.

'Oh, but it'll be good to have them back, won't it?' said Mrs Parvis. 'Not that one likes to mention too much of that sort of thing in front of poor Mr Brown. Of course, one can't hold it against him. It's just, he must have felt so *out* of it, stuck here while all our brave boys have been doing their bit for us.'

Dot thought of Mr Brown's two missing fingers. Sometimes in her memory, it was her faceless father who was two fingers short instead.

She wondered, if Mr Brown *were* able to get them back, would he want them, or had he now grown too accustomed to his hand the way it was?

3 A New Tweed Coat

'She's a scrappy little thing, isn't she?' said Mrs Parvis. 'Takes after her father, does she?'

She was discussing Dot.

Gloria shrugged. Dot fingered her victory badge and tried not to listen in case it seemed like prying.

'If you want my advice, lovie, you'll pop her down the Town Hall and find her a decent coat to wear. When you go to fetch her rations.'

Gloria and Dot went down to the Town Hall once a fortnight to collect Dot's vitamin ration. Two bottles of orange juice, opaque and brilliantly coloured, one of cod liver oil, translucent and greenish-gold. Before the tin victory brooch, these bottles of liquid strength were the only goods that Dot knew were hers alone, belonging to no grown-up. Gloria poured her a spoonful from each bottle every day and said that's why she was tough as old boots, because she always swallowed it down like a good girl. A previous landlady had tried to help herself to the orange juice to put in her gin. When Gloria complained, there'd been a tiff and they'd had to leave.

'You know I can't go buying her nothing!' Gloria said now about the coat.

'They won't ask for no clothing coupons down there,' said Mrs Parvis.

'It's not coupons I'm short of. They gave me all them extra ones for Baby's nappies what I never used.'

'Didn't you even get him a proper layette, the poor wee mite?'

'I'm not made of money, Mrs Parvis. I told you I got coupons coming out of my ears. It's cash we're stuck on.'

'At the Clothes Exchange, dear, you don't need no money down there. Nor coupons. It's meant for people like you what haven't got nothing left.'

Dot didn't like it when Mrs Parvis spoke in this way, as though they were dusty victims from under the rubble. Maybe they hadn't got any clothes, and they couldn't afford one of the nice rooms, and they didn't belong anywhere, but they had each other and they had Baby to visit each day.

'Women's Voluntary running it.'

'I know all about them,' said Gloria. 'Busybodies, the lot of them. Worse than Air Raid Wardens.'

'Beggars can't be choosers. Anyway, you never know, you might find something there. You want her to look as though you care, don't you? Besides she'll catch her death with just that little woolly cardy.'

'If you say so, Mrs Parvis. Try any dodge once,' said Gloria.

'By the by, you giving her her vitamins? Don't want her to go the way of Baby, do you now?'

'Interfering old bag,' muttered Gloria so that Mrs Parvis probably heard. But they set out for the Town Hall none the less.

'Matter of fact, Dot, what I really fancy you in is one of them nice Scottish tartan kilts like the princesses had when they was little. Remember them on their summer holiday? Matching check kilts, playing in the purple heather. With a nice fluffy jumper. Fair Isle, that's what they called it.'

The clerk behind the hatch asked for their empties before she'd hand over the new bottles but they hadn't got them. They were still half full back at their room.

'Try and remember next time,' the clerk snapped. 'We can't go wasting glass. Remember, we've all got to fight for the future now.'

'You don't say!'

Sometimes Dot wished Gloria wouldn't answer back to people in authority because then they noticed them more.

The hall where the Children's Clothes Exchange was

taking place was organized by another bossy lady in green uniform, sitting importantly behind a desk in the doorway.

'This is an *exchange*, not a rummage sale,' she said when she saw that Gloria had brought along no clothes to swap.

'Well I haven't got nothing to hand in, have I? And if I had she'd be wearing it. Then I wouldn't need to bring her up here, would I?'

The lady in green pursed up her lips. 'Oh, all right, in you go, but don't go taking too much. I know what some of you lot are up to.'

'Ta ever so,' said Gloria. 'She's got to look nice for when we go up the hospital to see my little boy.'

In a huge bare hall, trestle tables were heaped with children's garments and there was a thick, stifling smell in the air. Women in headscarves were sifting through the untidy muddle like rescue workers scrabbling in rubble for survivors while children stood by, waiting for the emergence of something to look at. Sometimes children grizzled, sometimes they wailed.

Dot didn't like the smell of old clothes nor of brick dust and escaping gas but she rarely wailed.

'Are they clean?' one woman asked, picking out a little coloured dress to measure up against her own child.

'I should think so too!' snapped the lady keeping order behind the table. 'They've all been fumigated quite properly under Ministry supervision.' But Dot could see how the lady herself wore white cotton gloves to handle the clothing, so as not to touch it directly.

Dot waited quietly till Gloria emerged from the jostling crowd holding up a fawn coat, triumphant like the A.R.P. men when they'd retrieved a live person, or even a dead one. Once Dot had seen a canary in a bent cage pulled out, black like a little sparrow from the ashes and soot, yet still singing even though its owner was gone.

'Real tweed. And look at that label!' said Gloria. 'Daniel Neal. That means it's quality. The princesses used to have their clothes from there. *By Appointment to Her Majesty*, it says.'

13

The coat smelled musty and the cuffs felt greasy. Dot didn't think the princesses had ever had greasy cuffs.

'I'd have preferred it pink, that's more feminine like, but them dull colours, that's just like the princesses used to wear.' It was double-breasted with two rows of pearl buttons up the front. Gloria buttoned Dot up.

'Well aren't you the one! All dressed up like the cat's dinner.'

Gloria seemed so pleased that Dot didn't like to say how constricting the coat felt round the neck.

'Here, I got you these too.' Gloria had two white woollen socks. 'Don't quite match, but near as makes no difference.' One was longer than the other and a different, more yellowy, shade of white. 'You're going to look a proper little madam. Nice white socks and a proper little coat. See, it's got velvet on it just like the princesses used to have when they was little. You're going to look too posh to go walking with me. People'll think I'm your nanny.'

Dot felt in the pockets. They had velvet flaps over them like letterboxes. She found a used tram ticket to Holborn in one and a little hanky scrumpled up in the bottom of the other. She smoothed it over with her hand. It was trimmed with a border of lace and printed with a pattern of flowers.

'Ooh, violets! Isn't that lucky! A hanky for you too. That's fine Swiss cotton, that is. When we get back I'll rinse it through. Then you can keep it in there so you've always got it.'

Gloria was always telling Dot she should try to hold on to things so she'd have them as keepsakes for ever. Yet Gloria herself never seemed to hold on to more than the bare essentials that they had in their two paper carriers. The only keepsakes Gloria had were her best peep-toe shoes and her little black hat with the veil.

'Funny, isn't it, how things just slip away without you noticing? Someone once gave me ever such a lovely little china cup when you was born, with pictures on it. Flowers and that. That was gone before you'd even learned to sit up by yourself.'

The violet-patterned handkerchief had some writing in the corner.

Dot asked, 'What's that say?'

' "Henrietta",' Gloria read it out for Dot. ' "Forbes-Read".'

'What's it mean?'

'That's a name tape. Though you'd have thought they'd have taken it off before bringing in their things. It's not very nice, leaving it on there, is it? Never mind, I'll unpick it when I wash it through for you.'

'No, leave it, please,' said Dot. 'I like it.'

She wondered what the coat's first owner was wearing now. Or perhaps it belonged to a child who was under rubble.

'Sent away to America more like,' said Gloria. 'Still, maybe she's left some of her luck behind in her pockets.'

When Dot went to bed that night, Gloria laid the fawn coat over the top of the blanket. It felt heavy.

'So as some of the luck'll spill out on you when you're asleep,' she said.

'Really?' said Dot.

' 'Course not, silly billy! Just having you on. It's to keep the cold out of your bones.'

As she waited for sleep, Dot thought she saw the face of the coat-owner gazing out of the dark with a complexion as pale and refined as tissue-paper.

4 The Day that Baby Went

Visiting Ward 3-South was built into Dot's life. Gloria disappearing between the double swing doors with the round port-hole windows too high to see through, and Dot in the dark brown corridor standing, standing, waiting, for however long it took.

Apart from that one time when Gloria went off instead to cheer the King, Dot couldn't remember a day when they hadn't been to visit whatever hospital he was in.

But today Gloria blundered out through the swing doors when she'd hardly been in there any time at all and looked like she was groping along in her sleep. Dot had seen people like that before, long ago. They hadn't been hurt, not so much as a graze on them, yet when the all-clear sounded, they came out of their buildings and stood on their street with blank eyes that seemed to stare inwards.

'That's him, then, all gone,' Gloria said, before a nurse came scurrying out through the doors, took her by the arm and led her back into the ward.

The long corridor was empty. Dot took a chance peek in through the crack between where the two doors met. It looked nice and peaceful in there. The floor was dark green and shiny like a sheet of still water, and everything else was white. The metal bedsteads were white, the cotton covers on them white, and the children lying straight and still wore white gowns. Every child had a bed or a cot to themselves. No sharing and rolling down into the dip in the middle.

Another nurse, older-looking and in blue, marched along the corridor. She snapped at Dot, 'What are *you* doing, hanging around here?'

16

'Waiting for my Mum,' said Dot. 'In there.'

'Are you indeed,' said the navy-blue nurse. Then, 'Ah, *I* see,' as though she knew something special. She hurried away through the swing doors, then out again to tell Dot, more kindly, that her brother had gone on a journey. 'A long journey. He won't be coming back.'

Dot thought that he must have been moved to a different hospital. She said, 'How far?' She wondered what number bus they'd have to get. If it was too far, they'd have to move lodgings again. Dot didn't want that.

'Why can't he stay in this hospital? He likes it here.'

The nurse said, 'Never mind, hen.' Then Dot understood what she'd meant. And Dot had a sinking feeling because she realized she'd known all along even though she hadn't wanted to.

That's what always happened to people you knew. Away they went and never came back. But Dot had thought it wouldn't ever happen to their baby. She'd hoped he was too young.

They left the hospital and went to wait for the bus. Gloria didn't pause to say anything to the cheery porter at the gates, nor did he call out to them. He was looking the other way, sorting mail.

Dot knew that Gloria was sad. She wasn't chatting to other people in the queue. Her red lipstick was smudged and she hadn't bothered to pin up her hair properly at the sides.

Dot wanted to make Gloria feel happy. She tugged at her hand. 'Shall we play princesses?' she whispered.

They would be young girls growing up at the palace, the princesses Elizabeth and Margaret.

Gloria took the part of the elder princess. 'Main thing is,' she used to explain, 'we have to act natural, because that's what they done, none of your fancy airs and graces. Just natural and nice, and ever so ladylike.'

Dot liked it when Gloria wanted to play. It felt like seeing a film happening round you. All Dot had to do was smile pleasantly and stand a little behind because, as Gloria

17

pointed out, Princess Margaret wasn't nearly as important as Princess Elizabeth and would never become a queen.

'And you watch out for the royal governess!' Gloria used to warn. 'Or you'll catch the sharp end of her tongue! She taught 'em how to behave, made 'em do their lessons at high desks. That's so they'd get used to the standing. Specially Princess Elizabeth. She has to do a lot of standing.'

'I wouldn't· ever want to be a princess,' Dot sometimes said, because she wanted so much to be one.

'Well that's all right, then, ain't it?' Gloria sometimes replied. 'Because you ain't never gonna have to be.'

But now she said, 'No, not just now, ducks.'

'D'you wanna play *Stars*, then?' Dot asked.

That was the other game Gloria liked. She chose the film and the parts they were to play. Sometimes she said she was Gloria Swanson. Sometimes Loretta Young. Or Ginger Rogers. Or Barbara Stanwyck. They had lovely exotic names. Gloria knew them all. But the films had strange names which didn't seem to Dot to mean anything. *And Now Tomorrow, Forever Young, Till Midnight Comes*. What sense was there in that?

Gloria had taken Dot to the cinema a few times. It was very dark. And when the stars' faces filled the whole screen so that you saw their huge lips close up like big pillows moving and their great teeth and their smooth matt skin filling the whole screen, it was frightening. The films Gloria liked were about love and people singing to each other. Sometimes though, there was just talking. Then Dot couldn't understand what was going on. Sometimes Gloria explained.

'See, she's lost her memory in a terrible storm. He's a stranger from out of town.'

'Who's that other lady?'

'She's pretending to love him. Really she's after him for his money.'

'What's going to happen?'

'Ssh, I don't know. That's why we're here. To find out.'

18

'When will it be over?'

'I said, ssh.'

The bus was a long time coming and Gloria wouldn't play anything, just stood there staring at nothing until finally she said, 'Now I ain't got him no more.'

'You got me,' said Dot.

Gloria blinked. 'That coat didn't have no luck left in it after all, did it?' Dot gave her the violet-patterned hanky that used to belong to Henrietta Forbes-Read to wipe her eyes.

'What are we going to do?' said Dot. If they stopped visiting the hospital every day, there wouldn't be anything left in life except a gaping crater of nothingness and broken bricks. Dot wanted to be back in their room at Mrs Parvis's. That was where they both felt safe. Gloria had always said so. 'You're always safe in a basement. They can't get you down there. Not unless it's a direct hit, then you've had it anyway. So long as someone knows you're down there and comes to dig you out, then a basement's always best, even if the rest goes down like a pack of cards.'

They didn't wait any longer for the bus. They walked all the way. Dot's legs ached. She wanted to sit down. Her shoelace came undone. She wanted to be carried.

'You're too old for all that now,' Gloria snapped. 'Don't push your luck.'

Being back in the basement didn't turn out to be any good after all. No sooner were they there than Gloria announced, 'We can't stay down here any more. It's got bad feelings for me, this room. And just when I thought everything was changing for the better. We'll tell her we're going away for a breather.'

'Why have we got to go?' Dot didn't want to have to go away somewhere. 'We're always having to move.'

'On a trip. There's this place I know,' said Gloria. 'She always said I could keep in touch.'

Dot wondered what sort of a trip, what sort of a place.

'Where? Why? What? Just don't ask me no more

questions, Dot. Can't you see, I've got to have time to get myself straight inside.'

Dot heard Gloria tell Mrs Parvis about what had happened. 'He was took quite sudden.'

'Pneumonia, I dare say,' said Mrs Parvis. 'Usually is. Don't suppose he had the strength left in that little body to fight back no more, though you'd have thought they could've saved him with these new pills they got. M and B, they're called. My sister's boy was saved with them. Did him a power of good. He had middle ear. His drum was pierced.'

'They said it was for the best,' said Gloria.

'And I dare say it was too,' said Mrs Parvis. 'From what you told me. Didn't stand a chance from the start. They don't, kids like that.'

'They gave him the oxygen, to help him breathe. But then they took it away, said it was blinding him. I wouldn't have minded him blind. Better than not at all.'

Mrs Parvis gave Gloria a pat on the shoulder and for once seemed almost friendly. 'You go off now and forget all about it. Don't bother about the rent if you haven't got it now, just so long as you pay me as soon as you get back.'

Dot didn't want to forget all about it. She wondered if it was all right for her to go on thinking about Baby. She wondered what the hospital would do with him. Where did dead babies go? But she knew she couldn't ask while Gloria was still getting herself straight inside.

Gloria put on her stockings, one coupon each, two for the pair and always kept for best, straightened the seams up the back, Vaselined her eyebrows, and put on her suede peep-toe shoes and her little black hat with the veil which usually lived in one of the paper carrier bags on the top of the shelf. She'd been married in that hat.

'Cost me my last five bob. Because I said to myself, even if you can't afford no frock, can't afford no party, can't afford no bouquet, at least you can have a new hat.'

By the time they reached the railway station, Dot realized she must have had time to get herself straight inside, for she seemed almost cheery again. But she was frightened of the station. It was too big, a great covered space where people strode backwards and forwards in a hurry. The space rattled with loud disconnecting sounds which echoed about so you couldn't tell which direction they were coming from.

'It's too big here,' said Dot.

She looked up at the curved glass roof overhead, so high and with pigeons on the inside, fluttering amongst the iron girders, trapped inside. The roof was too high and was partly made of glass. Dot didn't like the glass. Some of it was broken. When glass shatters it leaves jagged edges.

'They're trying to get out,' Dot said. 'They can't.'

'Who can't?'

'Them birds up there. They'll cut themselves.'

' 'Course they won't. They like it up there, it's cosy for them. That's their home, where they live.'

'Let's go back,' said Dot, tugging at Gloria's hand.

Crouching by the gas fire in the basement, staring into the redness of the flame until your cheeks burned and the shilling ran out, was safe. Listening to noises outside, yet not being part of them was safe too. Here was not safe.

'But we're going on a trip, lovie. You'll like it when you get there, honest. Come on, big smile now, give your face a joy-ride.'

Dot tried to smile but it wouldn't come. 'I don't like it here,' she said.

'But we ain't even there yet. It's only a railway station, pet,' said Gloria. 'That's just the noise of the loudspeakers.'

Dot knew about Underground stations. Once or twice they'd had to sleep down there, though not often because Gloria said it wasn't nice to be all pressed up against people you didn't know. And you might catch tuberculosis from their breath. But Dot couldn't remember ever being in a place like this. So high. So noisy. So much confused rushing about. Dot knew that when grown-ups started scurrying purposefully, something bad was about to happen, specially if you hadn't heard the siren.

21

' 'Course you have, pet,' said Gloria. 'That time we came down from Winfarthing-Fersfield, after seeing your old man.'

'Wasn't like this,' said Dot. She couldn't remember it at all. She just knew that a basement room was for sitting in, a children's ward for visiting, and railway stations had been prime targets for being bombed. She held more tightly to Gloria's hand.

'There's nothing to be frightened of, ducks. Not when there's all these nice people about.' So long as they weren't too close and breathing their germs on her, Gloria liked there to be people about. 'And she's ever such a nice lady we're going to see.'

'Who?'

'I told you. Mrs Hollidaye. Where I used to live, when they evacuated me the first time.'

Dot couldn't remember her.

' 'Course you can't remember, you was hardly even born, when we was there. But you remember me telling you about it.'

Dot shook her head.

'Her husband was a real gentleman, ever so brave. I liked him. But then he went and jumped out of a plane in France. He hadn't never even done it before. Got a medal for it.'

'Did he have his gas mask on?'

'How should I know? What kind of question is that?'

Dot wondered why it was braver to jump out of a plane than to lose two fingers in a factory.

'Mr Brown must have been quite brave,' she said. Why hadn't he been given a medal?

'Who's Mr Brown?'

'He didn't have to do it, did he?'

' 'Course not. He done it because he wanted to. He done it for his soldiers, to show them what they had to do. He was their padre like. Had a parachute on his back just like the rest, and holding out the holy cross in his hand. But the Germans went and got him.'

22

Dot wondered. Perhaps it was dying that was the bravest thing a person could do? So was Baby brave when he died? Or could dying only be brave if you were shot at?

'Derek's brave, isn't he?' she said.

But Gloria didn't hear, or anyhow didn't answer.

When Dot began to cry she wasn't sure if it was because of thinking about poor Mr Brown's two missing fingers or because she couldn't remember what her father's face looked like, or merely because of the alarming new orders about train departures cackling from the loudspeakers.

'I tell you what, pet, let's pop into the Buffet and get a nice cup of tea before the train goes. How about that, then?'

Dot liked sharing a cup of tea. Gloria drank first, from the top where it was scalding hot. Dot spooned up the bottom from where it was cool and milky.

5 A Trip on a Train

The compartment was fitted out with everything they would need to live there for ever. It was like having a perfect home of their own. They had their own windows with dark blue oil-cloth roller-blinds through which Dot could see into the compartment of the train alongside just like looking over at a next-door house.

Beneath the window was a useful fold-out table. There were brass ashtrays, coat-hooks, a mirror where Gloria would be able to do her hair, an overhead net to store things. The two rows of upholstered seats facing each other were like a pair of matching beds, one for each so they would not again need to share except when they wanted to.

'I like it here,' said Dot, stretching out along her bed while Gloria took off her hat and placed it carefully on the luggage rack. 'It's comfy.'

'We ain't there yet, pet. We ain't even started.'

Just as the train began to move, a soldier with a kit bag slung like a khaki corpse over his shoulder glanced into their compartment.

'Ooops-a-daisy,' he said. 'No smoker.'

Gloria pretended not to notice him. Usually she loved a good chat, specially with people from the services.

Overhead Dot noticed a row of shaded lamps each with its own switch. Gloria would be able to read her *Picturegoer* as late as she wanted without keeping Dot awake. Between the lamps, just as in a proper home, was a pair of framed photographs. Mrs Parvis had photographs in her parlour. Hers hung on picture hooks. These ones were screwed to the wall.

' *"Brighton and Hove Southern Railway"*,' Gloria read out.

' "*The Royal Promenade, Eastbourne.*" That's at the seaside. I'll take you there. One day. Maybe. Other one's Brighton. I never been to Brighton. Now sit still and stop hopping about, will you. Anyone'd think you was a flea on the organ-grinder's monkey.'

The windows were streaky like at the basement.

'We'd clean them windows,' Dot said. 'If this was our home, wouldn't we?'

First thing we'd do she thought, with a cloth and a big bucket of soapy water. So they'd sparkle. So you could see out any time you wanted.

Gloria closed the sliding door, pulled down the blinds, and switched off the six lamps which Dot had just put on.

'Can't see!' said Dot. 'I need to look out my windows!' She lifted the bottom corner of one of the blinds.

'Oi, don't lean out or you'll get smuts in your eye! You don't understand, it's better this way, love. You *will* behave proper when we get there, won't you? You won't go letting me down. Oh, I do hope you don't. Look at your face! You still got that hanky?'

It was in Dot's pocket, still scrumpled up, still waiting for its rinse through. Gloria wrapped a corner of it round her index finger, spat to make it wet, then dabbed at Dot's cheeks till they were sore.

'See, ducks, this Mrs Hollidaye what we're going to see, her clothes are that shabby, but she's like a real lady. She has these pearls round her neck. Wears them all the time, even when she's out digging. So I really want you to be like a proper sort of little girl. She's ever so posh, but she's ever so kind too. I want her to think we're *nice* people.'

'You *are* a nice person,' said Dot, though she was beginning to feel unsure about it. Nothing in the world was ever certain or fixed, things changed easily and when least expected. She thought she'd found the perfect place to live, yet already it was slipping away and this cosy compartment was only a stage on to something else. So who were the nice people? Was the King a nice person and the princesses?

' 'Course royalty is!' said Gloria, shocked. 'Goes without

saying. Now your socks.' She reached down to take off Dot's shoes, then her socks, one long, one not so long, one greyish white, the other a different kind of fawnish white. She turned them inside out, returned them to Dot to put on with the insides now on the outside. White socks never stayed clean. It was all very well for the princesses. There probably hadn't been much dust lying around in a palace.

'Grey socks are better,' said Dot. They didn't show scuff marks at all.

'See, I don't want Mrs Hollidaye to go thinking you're riff-raff. I don't want her to go getting any wrong ideas about what's become of me.'

The train was moving fast. Gloria said, 'Come over here now. Lay in my lap. Suck your thumb, there's a love.'

Dot looked at it and was surprised to see how dirty it had become. She inspected the fingers and thumb on her other hand. These too had become smudged with dirt, and the velvet cuffs of her coat, and everything in the compartment was flecked with specks of greasy black which came off on to you the moment you touched them. She wondered if this coat had ever been on a train before, when it had belonged to the other child.

'Yes, *please* do,' said Gloria.

She pulled Dot onto her knee. Being cradled against her mother's soft warm body, Dot tried to feel like a baby, to remember what she had seen through the crack in the double doors as Gloria had cradled Baby against her while the nurses gathered round with protective outstretched arms.

Sometimes Gloria was so strange. First she wanted Dot to be nice, next she wanted her to put a filthy thumb in her mouth and suck it.

Obediently, Dot did as Gloria asked, gripping her thumb between her front teeth to prevent it slipping out.

'Where we going?' Dot asked, her thumb still lying firmly on her tongue like Gloria wanted it.

'And don't talk no more.'

So Dot whispered it.

'Sssh. You gotta be like my baby.'

Dot sat bolt upright. 'I can't be your baby! You said I was too big to be carried. I don't want to be no baby! I don't want to be blind and dead.'

'Please, ducky. Be a baby for Mum. Just on the train, till the man's been past. See, I didn't have the money to get no ticket for you.'

Gloria took from her bag a little blanket made of coloured squares that a long-ago lady in a shelter had knitted for Baby before he was born.

'Baby's blanket!' said Dot in surprise. 'You brought it!'

Gloria wrapped it gently around Dot's head and shoulders, pulling it well forward over her face.

'Now I can't even see,' said Dot.

'Just till after the bloke's been along. I told you, I haven't got no ticket for you.'

Although not exactly dark, nor scary because Gloria was holding her tenderly, it was stuffy under the blanket and irritating to be covered over when you wanted to look out. Dot sucked away on her thumb.

'Can I come out yet?'

'No, ssh. He's just coming.'

Dot heard the compartment door open. A draught of cold air blew in. Dot heard the man ask for Gloria's ticket, felt the movement as Gloria reached for her purse.

'Taking me little one down to the country to see her Nan,' she heard Gloria say, then the click-clack of the ticket-clipper before the man closed the door and they were alone again.

Dot said, 'Who's my Nan?'

'Your Nan died years ago.'

'But you said we're going to see my Nan.'

'Oh, that. That was to stop him asking nosy questions, like how old you was. But it's all right. I don't think he was that bothered. You look small enough.'

Dot pushed back the blanket, slid off Gloria's lap and moved back to sit by her window. She lifted the bottom of the blind.

'That's right. You take a peek. That's the real country-side out there. Ain't it lovely? Full of animals and that.'

'What kind of animals?'

'Aw, I dunno,' Gloria said vaguely. 'Cows and bulls. That sort of thing.'

The next-door train had been left far behind. The houses had all gone too. There was nothing out there now. No walls, no roads, no buildings. No red buses, no red letterboxes, no red telephone boxes. No iron railings. No pavements, no front doors, no streets, no nothing and it was growing dark as the black nothingness dashed past the window.

'I want to go back. I changed my mind. I don't like it no more.'

'Do stop that crying!' Gloria snapped. 'It makes your eyes all red. And now look at your face. All messed up again after I just cleaned you up! Take a look at it!'

She held Dot up to the mirror and Dot saw the greyish rivulets where tears had run down her cheeks and been smudged to grey by her hands.

She wondered how clean tears could make a person's skin go dirty.

'I told you you'd got to try and keep yourself looking nice for Mrs Hollidaye,' said Gloria. 'You wash clean and dry dirty, that's always been your trouble.'

6 A Walk in the Night

'Wakey-wakey! Come on, pet, you're holding up production!'

Dot felt herself being nudged awake, saw Gloria seize their two paper carriers, and they scrambled off the train at a dark station in the countryside.

Then they started walking. The track felt soft and slithery but in the dark she couldn't see what it was she was stepping on.

'Come on, pet. Keep up. Or I'll lose you.'

There were traps to catch them along the way. The heel of Gloria's peep-toe shoe caught in a hole. Then the sleeve of Dot's coat was clawed at by a long briar.

Dot knew it was more dangerous than anything in London, even during blackout and raids.

Dot had heard often enough how careless talk costs lives, how even walls have ears. 'It's ever so dark round here,' she whispered. Somebody in the blackness around them was bound to be listening.

'You can say that again,' said Gloria.

'You said it'd be *nice*.'

'Well I was wrong, weren't I? I must have forgot.'

In London, the big plane tree stuck in the pavement outside Mrs Parvis's house had three white rings painted round its black trunk so people could see it even in the dark. Here you couldn't tell if there were any obstacles in the way, and there were no pavements either. Instead they were surrounded by ambiguous smells of unrecognizable growing things that had rotted and died, of living creatures that were scarcely human, hairy and fleshy. There were unknown sounds of subhuman things proceeding relentlessly forward, stopping, retrenching, to proceed onward again.

Dot knew it must be tanks. She had never seen a tank close to. But she had seen them on the newsreel before the big film, creaking and groaning across the land, their great limbless, legless form crushing and grinding all that was in their way.

Gloria said, 'That's never tanks. That's trees making a noise. Or maybe the hedges.' But now she was whispering too and Dot knew that she didn't know what was out there with them either.

Dot tried not to think of Hitler, nor of Dick Barton Special Agent, nor of the Fifth Columnists, nor of those giant nuns with rifles and huge booted feet beneath their long black skirts who were enemy soldiers in disguise. Yet all the most unspeakably wicked men in the world, who caused havoc and lurked in dim places ready to pounce again, came surging into her mind. Mrs Parvis said Hitler hadn't really taken the poison in his bunker. She said that had been his double and he'd got away scot-free to come to live in the last country in the world where people would think of looking for him.

'Don't be silly, ducks, that's all over now.'

People were always saying things were over. But as Dot knew, it sometimes turned out they weren't. And in a way one didn't want things to be over, for the uncertain future was more unsettling than the unexplained past.

Dot wished that the metal caps on Gloria's high-heels wouldn't make such a tapping as they walked. She wondered what had been the use of all that trying to get clean on the train if they were now lost in a place where nobody would ever find them, not even when something happened and they disappeared for ever. If only they'd stayed in the little home on the train. If only they'd never left the basement with the empty meat-safe hanging outside the window.

She heard heavy breathing like panting. It seemed to follow her like Hitler, Himmler, and the marching white faces of all the dead men.

'Just an animal, I expect,' Gloria whispered. 'You get all

30

sorts. That's what it's for, the country. They live in the fields.'

'What are they doing?'

'How should I know? You'll be the death of me with all your questions.'

'They'll have finished tea by now, won't they?' Dot said.

'Who?'

'Back at Mrs Parvis's.'

By now Dot would have had her dab with the damp corner of a towel at the sink on the landing. She'd be tucked beneath the blanket and the heavy coat and watching Gloria put on her make-up before she went out. Once in a while she went to a social club for air pilots who'd been in hospital. She didn't take Dot.

'You wouldn't like it, pet. Some of them don't look too good, not after they been burned like that, specially when it's their features what have gone. That's worse than legs.'

'Are we nearly there?'

The thin string handles of the carrier bag cut deep into the palm of Dot's hand. Gloria kissed it better and carried both bags.

When Dot began to stumble and fall over with tiredness, Gloria gathered her up and carried her too.

Clinging piggy-back to her mother's back, Dot felt the curtain of bunchy black net on the side of Gloria's hat flick at her face. She felt the two paper carriers swinging where Gloria had put them over her wrists. Dot's eyes were growing used to the dark just like they had to in the shelter when the warden's lamp went out. Now Dot could see the shapes of trees beside the track, of fences, of a white gate. There were no tanks, no Fifth Columnists disguised as Sisters of Charity. They were going up a stony drive. Gloria was walking faster, almost striding on her high heels as though she had finally refound her way.

'Here it is, then,' said Gloria, setting Dot down.

'What's this, then? Another blooming hospital?' She saw the dark looming bulk of a large building.

' 'Course it's not.'

31

'Looks like it. It's got windows all over.' She didn't want to be left to stand alone in some dark night-time corridor.

'You got hospitals on the brain. Come on, follow me. Round the back.'

Dot clutched tight to Gloria's coat as they made their way through the dark rustling leaves of some tall shrubs. Across silent grass, showed the faint light from a downstairs window.

'That's her in her drawing-room,' said Gloria. 'This way now. Side door'll be open.'

Gloria led them along a brick path, across a cobbled courtyard, past outhouses and a dripping water butt, then into the big house and along many passages.

Dot knew what was going to happen. She was going to be left in the care of a woman she didn't know, just as she'd been left with them before. 'Only an hour,' Gloria would say. 'She won't be no trouble to you. She's ever so good. Shan't be gone long.' And then the hour would turn into a long space of empty time, then into a whole evening, once even into an entire night before Gloria came back.

Now that they hadn't Baby to visit any more, all that was bound to start again.

Dot thought, I won't let her. I'll stick with her. I'm all she's got now.

Gloria knocked on a panelled door before pushing it open.

'Here we are, then, Mrs Hollidaye. Dot and me, come to visit you,' she said brightly.

'Come on, come in. And who have we here?'

'It's me, Gloria.'

The large room was lit by a paraffin lamp on a table. Two grey-haired ladies sat either side of a fire eating green soup from wide dishes on their knees.

The fire was burning large branches of wood, some still with twigs attached like fingers.

'Don't they have no gas?' said Dot. 'Them's trees they're burning in there.'

'Ssh,' said Gloria.

'Why, Gloria, my dear!' said one of the ladies, putting aside her soup-dish and hurrying across the wide room to welcome them almost, but not quite, as though she had been expecting them.

'There, see, Dot,' said Gloria. 'What did I say? Told you she'd be pleased, didn't I?'

'Why it's a delightful surprise! We were only thinking of you the other week. Weren't we, Lilian?'

The other lady went on spooning up her soup and Dot noticed how frequently she missed her mouth. She had a brow so low that her hair seemed to begin sprouting from just above her eyes which moved independently. She appeared to be looking in two directions at once and Dot couldn't tell whether or not she was being stared at.

She remembered Hitler's eyes which Mrs Parvis had once said were hypnotic. 'Must have been, otherwise why would all them nice Germans have done all them wicked things what he told them?'

Dot avoided the danger of the swivelling eyes in case they had the same compelling powers. She looked down at the patterned rugs on the floor and edged in more closely behind Gloria, gripping her skirt.

'So this is your little Dorothy?'

'That's right.' Gloria pushed Dot forward. 'This is her. Large as life and twice as natural.'

Mrs Hollidaye bent down and held out her hand. 'Why, how *do* you do, my dear,' she said.

'Shake hands nicely,' Gloria hissed in Dot's ear. 'Show her you're pleased to be here.'

'But I ain't.'

'My poor dears, come and warm yourselves by the fire. You must be most awfully tired. Why, Gloria my dear, you should have called from the station. We could have harnessed up the goat-cart and come and fetched you. At least the little girl could have ridden. Never mind, the main thing is you're here now.'

She pushed two dogs off an armchair.

33

'Come, darlings, make room for our visitors while I go and fetch them some supper.'

Dot remembered how Mrs Parvis had said dogs were insanitary vermin and had no place in the war effort and the Chinese were quite right to eat them.

'I believe there's a little soup left. Runner bean. All our own. We salted down simply pounds and pounds. And Lilian, look sharp. Help the little girl out of her coat. Poor child, looks more dead than alive.'

Dot felt herself freeze with fear as the swivel-eyed Lilian lurched towards her, arms outstretched, to try to remove her coat.

'Don't mind her,' Gloria hissed in Dot's ear. 'She's just a bit mental. Always has been. Don't mean no harm.'

Dot held her arms stiff as bayonets, for she knew it would be safer to keep her coat on, then they might not have to stay so long.

In the night, Dot heard the low thudding of explosions on the ground somewhere in the faraway distance and knew there must be a raid on. She had a sinking feeling. The grown-ups were wrong as usual. The war had come back, just like she knew it would. Yet she wasn't afraid and didn't even bother to open her eyes to find out if she would have to get up and run with Gloria for the shelters. She couldn't remember where she was, nor why, yet for some reason which she didn't understand, she felt they were safe here.

7 A Morning in the Country

Dot was surprised to find herself wearing a large pink woollen nightgown with embroidered collar whose gathered sleeves were so long that her hands were lost. Somebody must have undressed her the night before. It couldn't have been Gloria, for Gloria knew that Dot always slept in her vest and knickers.

Dot was in a wide high bed with white sheets, two pillows, two blankets and an eiderdown. Dot saw the curly mass of Gloria's dark hair lying on the pillow of a similar but separate bed alongside.

The room was like the train compartment again, their two matching beds, windows on two sides, blinds *and* curtains, pictures on the walls, a mirror and a place to hang clothes, but everything bigger, and they weren't travelling, and there was more light in the room. Blue light, and silver and bronze, streamed and bounced and danced through tall windows.

Across the gap between the beds, Dot whispered her mother's name.

'All present and correct,' Gloria mumbled, then rolled back to sleep.

A soft animal noise like gargling Dot thought at first must be Gloria's breathing. Then she saw that it was a grey bird like a station pigeon, yet not trapped beneath a glass roof but sitting freely outside amongst fluttering leaves.

In London colours were red and black. Here Dot saw that green and blue were the colours of the outside world. Green leaves festooned the window, green trees, green ground beyond, giving way to the blue. Blue distant trees, blue faraway hedges, rounded blue hills of the horizon millions of miles away. Dot thought, if only noble eight-fingered Mr Brown could have this outside his window. Better than a view of cardboard panes and the next-door privies.

There were toys in one corner of the big bedroom. Whose toys? Dot slid down from the high bed and sat on the carpet and looked at a wooden dolls' house, a painted rocking horse, but she didn't touch. They weren't hers and she knew there was always a danger in wanting other peoples' things for oneself. Like looters after a big raid who tried to steal the mangled possessions of shattered houses. Like Hitler who wanted all the countries of the world for himself. Even when the first owners were crushed and dead, their things were not for you.

Dot peered in through the tiny curtained windows of the dolls' house and saw quiet furnished rooms, the playroom, kitchen, parlour, waiting to be lived in, a table set for tea, beds to be slept in, armchairs to be sat on. She hoped that the child to whom this home belonged would let her stay and watch him playing.

But a thump at the door made her scramble back up on to the bed for safety. Gloria from under her covers, mumbled sleepily, 'That's only Loopy Lil, pet. Not to worry.'

The lady with the upright hair who Gloria said had a screw loose, clattered into the bedroom holding out a steaming jug on a tray.

Dot thought it must be tea. She'd have liked a nice cup of milky tea. But they had no cups to drink from. So she shook her head. 'No, thanks,' she said.

But Gloria said, 'That'll be the hot water, pet. For washing yourself.'

'We don't do that,' said Dot.

'Well, you do here.'

Reluctantly, Dot slid down from the bed while Loopy Lil beamed kindly, eyes swivelling in all directions and tried to help wash Dot's face at the wash-stand and brush her hair.

'Don't usually,' Dot muttered to Gloria. 'Thursdays.

36

That's our day.' Thursdays, half past five until six o'clock, was when they had the use of Mrs Parvis's bathroom and as much warm water as trickled from the gas geyser into the tub. Usually enough for Gloria to shampoo her hair, for both of them to swish around in shallow tepid water, followed by their underclothes.

'Well you ain't at Mrs P's now, are you?' said Gloria crossly. 'Washing hands, face, and behind your ears, that's what Mrs Hollidaye likes so you'll just do it. Right?'

She pummelled the two soft pillows into shape and lay down to sleep again.

'I'm keeping my coat on,' said Dot. A person felt safer if they kept their possessions close by them. 'And I won't stay,' she added as Loopy Lil reached out to take her hand and lead her downstairs.

'Nobody says you got to stay. But right now, you can just trot along and leave me a bit of peace to get some kip while I got the chance. I tell you, it's no laugh sharing with a kid what kicks and turns in her sleep week after week.' Gloria rolled over, pulling the covers up to her head.

'I tell you, you ain't leaving me here!' Dot shouted at the hump in the pink satin eiderdown. 'And I ain't leaving you neither!'

'Nobody's leaving nobody,' said Gloria from under the covers. 'You dig in and fill your boots while you can. And you don't forget to mind your blooming manners while you're at it.'

So Dot kept her coat on at breakfast-time but Mrs Hollidaye didn't seem to mind. She was busy stirring the porridge over an open wood range.

'Ah, Dorothy, my dear,' she said. 'I hope you've a good country appetite. What do you like best of all for your breakfast?'

Dot had no idea. At Mrs Parvis's you didn't choose. It was always the same—bread and dripping or, when the bread was very old, blackish toast and dripping.

Mrs Hollidaye said, 'Today, Miss Lilian is starting off with porridge and honey, aren't you, my dear?'

On the table was a vase of flowers, a square honeycomb oozing liquid honey from its wax holes onto the dish, three jars of jam, each one a different colour of dark red, and a jug with a muslin cloth over the top. The cloth was sewn with coloured glass beads round the edge.

'That's to stop the flies falling into the milk,' Mrs Hollidaye explained.

Loopy Lil grinned and Dot saw she didn't understand much of anything that other people said.

'Miss Lilian has an appetite fit for the good trooper that she is. Lilian, as you can see, was not gifted by our dear Lord, with either beauty or brains, but with a willing heart. Weren't you, Lilian?'

Loopy Lil beamed with pleasure but said nothing as she watched Mrs Hollidaye fill her bowl to the brim.

Dot said, 'In London, where I live, we don't have flies.' She was going to explain, too, how the milk came in glass bottles on a cart pulled by a brown horse, and how sometimes the horse left steaming heaps of brown, oval-shaped droppings in the road which people ran out to scoop up with coal shovels and take for their vegetable plots. But she remembered in time that Gloria had warned her to mind her P's and Q's, so she said nothing.

'And Lilian is my right-hand man. I don't know what we'd have done without her in those dark years. Always here to keep up our spirits, weren't you, my dear? She came with the rest of the evacuees, didn't you, Lilian? Will you try a little porridge with some honey, Dorothy, my dear? It's from our own bees. Some people say you can actually taste the clover in it. Or cream? They're not really allowed to make it down at the farm. Agricultural emergency committee still haven't lifted the ban. But this little bit they don't know about. Your mother was among the first batch of evacuees, too, like Lilian. But she just couldn't take to it. Village life is rather different from London. Newly wed she was and pretty as a picture.'

Lil swirled her eyes across the table before tucking in.

'And you mustn't mind if I take mine standing up, and

with a pinch of salt. Because of my Scottish blood. Then I can keep an eye on the eggs.'

Mrs Hollidaye was unlike Mrs Parvis or any of the other people Dot had been left with. Although sometimes Mrs Parvis talked *about* Dot, she rarely spoke *to* her, except to scold or reprimand, whereas Mrs Hollidaye went on talking cheerfully to Loopy Lil and to Dot even though neither replied.

'Or if you don't care for the porridge, there's some of these new *Post Toasties*. Such a nice young American brought them for us. Though I'm afraid Miss Lilian and I didn't think a lot of them, did we, Lilian? But do try them if you'd like. It says they don't need any cooking but I rather wonder. Perhaps with a little fruit?'

She passed a dish of scarlet berries in scarlet juice to Dot.

'Only bottled. The fresh ones are long since gone. But they're from the garden and they really are rather good. And then when all the others went,' Mrs Hollidaye carried on talking as she removed Loopy Lil's empty porridge bowl and replaced it with a plate piled high with toast, 'Lilian was the only one who stayed. You were from the institution weren't you? For people of diminished responsibility. They tried to put some of them into the Land Army, but Lilian wasn't quite up to it, were you, my dear?'

Dot wondered what an institution was. She said, 'Up London, we have the national orange juice on a teaspoon.' She didn't mention the cod liver oil.

'So how would you like your egg, my dear? Boiled, poached, scrambled. Lilian's having hers soft-boiled today, aren't you, dear? The hens have been doing frightfully well. I rather think they must have known you were coming. I don't suppose you have many eggs.'

Loopy Lil's cooked egg sat, still in its shell, in a small china cup with a spoon lying beside it. Dot had not seen an egg served up like that before. 'Up London,' she said, 'we get eggs all the time. But we do them different.'

Dot wasn't allowed into Mrs Parvis's kitchen except at the regulation meal-times and she wasn't sure about how food was prepared, but she was pretty certain that when Mrs Parvis cooked what was called a nice egg-dish, it was made from an orange coloured powder spooned up from a deep cylindrical tin. Dot wondered how Loopy Lil was going to eat this kind of egg.

'Hit him!' Loopy Lil cried suddenly, attacking the brown rounded shell with the tiny spoon.

Dot was surprised. It was the first time she'd heard her speak.

'She used to pretend her egg was Adolf Hitler,' said Mrs Hollidaye. 'Specially when we had those dreadful incendiary bombs dropping on the roof. It made Lilian feel a lot better in the morning, didn't it, dear?'

'Hit him, hit him!' Loopy Lil repeated till the top of her egg was open and yellow yolk pouring down the side.

Dot was pleased. Next time she had a nightmare, she would try imagining smashing, like eggs, the faceless looters and killers of her dreams.

'Maybe you could manage a little bit of bread and butter?' said Mrs Hollidaye, cutting and spreading a small slice. But Dot couldn't.

'Lovely fresh butter from the herd down at Mrs Elphinstone's. We'll walk over later, shall we, and catch a look at the milking? Can you taste the clover in it? And a nice little bit of our plum jam? We managed to get some sugar last month, didn't we, Lilian?'

Loopy Lil smiled and nodded.

Loopy Lil, even if she was mental, seemed a good safe person to be near.

'Though do watch out for the stones, won't you, my dear? They're rather dangerous if swallowed. And you don't want a plum tree growing up inside you, do you now?'

There were some things about the country that were difficult to get used to. Flies in the milk, clover in the butter, stones in the jam. Why should people in the country have these in their food?

Perhaps it was for the same reason that Mrs Parvis, so Gloria claimed, put crushed up egg-shells into powdered egg so that the lodgers would think they were eating something which they weren't.

'Never mind, my dear,' said Mrs Hollidaye. 'It takes time to build a country appetite. But we'll see if we can't lend you one before too long.'

Gloria had told Dot she was to fill her boots. Here was all this food on the table and Dot unable to swallow it down. She didn't want Gloria to be angry.

'Up London, where I live,' she said, 'we have bananas.'

'Why, do you now. Fancy that!' said Mrs Hollidaye.

Dot didn't know what a banana tasted like, though she'd heard Mrs Parvis talk about them often enough.

'D'you know, my dear,' said Mrs Hollidaye. 'Down here we haven't set eyes on a banana for years! I must say I've almost forgotten what they look like. Though my son, that's my eldest, in the Royal Navy, wrote that he has them in the Pacific.'

'Up London,' said Dot, 'we have them any time. Ain't even on ration coupons. Bananas is so cheap, Mrs Parvis says, they're giving them away with a pound of tea.'

'Why, isn't that splendid of them!' said Mrs Hollidaye.

8 Country Appetites

Halfway through the morning, once the hens had been fed, and the tomatoes in the greenhouse watered, it was time for another meal. Mrs Hollidaye called it elevenses.

Dot sat in her coat at the kitchen table and watched Mrs Hollidaye heaping thick slices of bread spread with yellow butter on to a plate while Loopy Lil set out pretty teacups patterned with roses on to matching saucers.

'You get ever such a lot of meals out here, don't you?' Dot said. 'Up London, we don't do this one.' All things were done differently in London. 'Up London,' Dot explained, 'we waits for our High Tea what Mrs Parvis makes till evening when the real people get back from their work. And Mr Brown has to have his straight off, no hanging about, because he wants to be an engineer, so he goes to night school. Mrs Parvis says he'll never make it. I know he will. He's ever so nice.'

On the dresser, Dot noticed a framed picture of a man in uniform. It was a black and white photograph which had been partially tinted with pastel colours so that though the young man's face was paper-white, his eyes were sky-blue and his medal ribbons bright as a rainbow.

Dot said, 'Your husband was ever so brave, weren't he? That's what Gloria says. That him, up there?'

'Do you know, it almost could be? Actually, that's another of my sons. In the Merchant Navy. Though people do say he's very like my husband.'

'Has he had it too, your boy there?'

'Not as far as I know, my dear. Though I must admit, we'll be glad when it's all over in the Far East and they can come back safe and sound.'

So it wasn't over yet. Dot had been right all along and Mrs Parvis wrong when she'd insisted that it was all over bar the shouting.

'Is he brave too?'

'Well there's so many different and wonderful ways of being brave, aren't there, my dear? That's the admirable way our good Lord arranged it, didn't he? So that everybody can have a stab at it. Even Miss Lilian has shown great fortitude in her own way.'

Loopy Lil was arranging and rearranging the teacups on their matching saucers.

'And your mother too is a most courageous young woman, isn't she? The way she's carried on.'

Dot wished she knew what it felt like to be brave, and wondered if she'd ever get the chance to find out. She wondered if eating when you didn't feel hungry was brave. She wondered if her father was brave. Was he a secret hero and was that why Gloria never talked about him?

She said, 'I think maybe my old man had a stab at it.'

The pale young sailor in the silver frame stared serenely out across the wide spaces of the kitchen with faraway forget-me-not eyes. Dot tried to remember her father's face from the brownish photo which Gloria kept in her handbag. She wished she could recall it more clearly. Even when she had the picture in front of her, she seemed only to see the flat bloodless paper. She wished her father was like this young man who sat in his own shrine on a country kitchen dresser amongst used OHMS envelopes and sprigs of dried white heather.

She said, 'We don't ever talk about my old man. But I think he liked bananas.'

A group of men and women came in to share the meal called elevenses. They had muddy boots which they kicked against the kitchen step, and muddy hands which they washed at the sink. One wore a sack round his shoulders like a shawl, another had it round her waist as an apron. They didn't sit but stood around the table. The china tea-cups seemed too dainty in their dark working hands. There

43

wasn't much talking between them, apart from pleases and thankyous when Dot heard how two of them spoke awkwardly with unfluent foreign accents.

The huge kitchen suddenly seemed too crowded. Dot felt the room lurch away, while the milk jug with its bead-decorated muslin cover, the fly-paper dangling from the lamp above the table, the rosy faces of the gathered people flew round through the air. Dot knew from their voices that those two young men who'd been working in the fields must be prisoners.

'You all right, my dear?' she heard Mrs Hollidaye say.

Them's Germans, Dot wanted to say but the words wouldn't come out.

'She's too hot, poor little scrap, in that tight coat,' said the woman in the sacking apron. Loopy Lil clucked anxiously around like a pigeon.

Mrs Hollidaye led Dot outside. 'Of course it's not your coat. You keep your coat on if you want to. It's eating. That's the trouble. We've got all the wrong food for you and you're just not used to it, are you? But I dare say you like apples. Come along, we'll go and find the very nicest apple there is for you.'

'I ain't never met a German before,' Dot said. 'Not close to.'

'Poor boys. Little more than children when they first arrived. They're just yearning to be home.'

This wasn't how Mrs Parvis used to speak of the enemy.

'One of them plays the piano most beautifully. They used to let him up here to practise from time to time.'

The apple room was dim and scented with a mysterious sweetness like the breakfast honey. Apples of many shades of yellow and red, brown and gold were laid out on yellowed newspaper, line after line, row upon row, on broad slatted shelves.

'Don't they give such a lovely smell!' said Mrs Hollidaye. 'They seem to get better and better.' She picked over the nearest of the apples, taking out three which had small brown marks.

'Those'll do nicely for the compost,' she said, then chose a dark gold one for Dot. 'We call this one a Russet. Have a try. They do seem to be lasting awfully well. Even better this year than last, though maybe that's just an illusion. For I heard *such* an interesting talk on the wireless. It seems we're all losing our taste for sweet things because of the shortages. What do you think?'

Dot bit through the taut and burnished skin of the apple into juicy flesh. The crunchy texture was like a raw potato she had once stolen from Mrs Parvis's vegetable rack. But the taste was refreshingly sweet. She wondered if this might be anything like the bananas that Mrs Parvis said were so exceptional.

But when she swallowed, the first mouthful of crisp apple hurt her throat so much she almost cried.

Mrs Hollidaye had already warned about plum trees growing inside you. Could the same thing happen with a single bite from an apple?

9 St Michael and the Angels

Mrs Hollidaye said, 'Would you like to come with me, Dorothy, to help with the flowers?'

What did she mean by that? Flowers didn't need helping. They just were.

'For a little run in the Ford.'

'Dunno about that,' said Dot. She was used enough to being left behind while Gloria went off, but it seemed more dangerous to do it the other way around, for her to leave Gloria behind.

'Sleep,' said Mrs Hollidaye. 'That's the best thing for her.'

Dot clutched at the cuffs of her coat but even the familiar softness of worn velvet was not reassuring.

'Dunno if I'm allowed. See, we don't go about in cars, not up London.'

Then in case she had given an impression that London was not as good as here, she added, 'But there's plenty of cabs.' She couldn't remember having actually been in one and anyway, they rarely came past Mrs Parvis's lodgings. 'Buses too. We have lots of buses up London. And Shanks's pony.'

'It isn't far, just down to the village and back. I have to take Mrs Squirrel. For her legs. Nurse Willow, that's our district nurse, lovely lady, member of our Mother's Union, holds surgery in the village hall. We have a special petrol allowance for that. It's not unlike a Red Cross run. So I always take my flowers for the altar at the same time. And pick up the groceries. Saves Mr Bob making the trip with the cart.'

'No, I ain't leaving her behind all on her own,' said Dot.

'You got to understand, if anything went wrong, then my name's mud.'

'We shan't be gone long. And Miss Lilian will be here to take her a nice little something on a tray if she wakes before we're back. Won't you, Lilian?'

Loopy Lil clattered at the sink in the back scullery.

'Oh, heck. Might as well.'

'Splendid, my dear. Then you hop in the back to keep the dogs company for me.'

It was more exciting and comfortable to travel in the back of a Ford car than on any part of a bus, even top front. Dot sat with the yapping dogs on either side licking at her hands. The basket of flowers was on the shelf behind them. Not made of coloured crêpe paper, faded, dusty and crinkled on bent wire stems like Mrs Parvis had in her parlour. But alive and dark and greenish, fragile and fragrant, dew on the petals and the crushed stems dripping with sap.

'Those long ones have a lovely scent, don't they?' said Mrs Hollidaye over her shoulder. 'I'm not sure if the purple ones are my favourite, or the more blue colour.'

She drove to a cottage where she helped an old woman bent in half like a crooked stump into the front passenger seat.

Dot tried to imagine that the two women in front were her footmen and she was one of the royal princesses, preferably Margaret because she wouldn't have to be queen which would be quite a responsibility if you thought about it, going for a drive in a carriage with her regal dogs and her regal flowers. Then she realized she didn't have to pretend to be anyone going anywhere when she already was herself going for a real drive in a car with two dogs beside her and fresh flowers behind.

It wasn't far. The bent lady with the bad legs was helped out. Mrs Hollidaye parked beside a stone cross, under which lay a brown dog sleeping. Mrs Hollidaye adjusted her hat-pin, gathered up the flowers and took Dot's hand firmly in hers. She paused by the brown dog on the ground.

47

'Why, here's Mr Honeysett's old Bess,' she said, bending down to stroke the dog's muzzle.

Dot thought how strange it was to be able to recognize a person's dog even when the person wasn't there, and then to know the dog's name. It wasn't like that in London. People didn't even know most other people's names let alone their dogs'. In fact, Dot wasn't at all sure if the dogs in London had names. Dogs' names wasn't something Mrs Parvis had yet spoken about.

'Dear old thing. She must be thirteen at least. That's about eighty in dog years.'

Mrs Hollidaye's dogs were left inside the car bobbing up at the rear window.

'I'm afraid their noses are a little out of joint,' said Mrs Hollidaye. 'Never mind. They'll just have to learn.'

The old dog on the ground yawned and seemed almost to smile at them.

'Up London,' said Dot, 'we don't have dogs so much.' She wished they did. It would be good to be greeted as you walked along by smiling creatures lying along the pavements. It would give Mr Brown a surprise when he went to night school.

In the village shop, Mrs Hollidaye introduced Dot to the man in a brown overall who stood behind the wooden counter.

'Good morning, Mr Bob,' she said. 'This is a young friend, Dorothy. She's come to visit us from London.'

'From London!' said the grocer. He made it seem important and special. 'Well, just fancy that! She must have seen a few sights in her time.'

A lady in a black straw hat, who was being weighed out a pound of grits by the grocer's assistant, overheard.

'A tiny child from London!' she repeated. 'Why, the poor creature! Oh, you little angel!' She darted over to embrace Dot so tightly that she couldn't breathe.

Dot had never been hugged by a stranger. Mrs Parvis gave no sign of being interested in her, let alone liking her enough to want to touch her.

'What *can* we give the little child?' said the lady. 'Just think what she must have been through! If only there were a little chocolate bar we could give her. Do you remember those peppermint creams we used to be able to get? Mr Bob, you must have *something* under the counter?'

'What Dorothy needs is a breath or two of good fresh air,' said Mrs Hollidaye sharply. 'And that's exactly what we can give her. To put a few roses back in her cheeks.'

'The little lamb,' said the lady.

After the shop, Mrs Hollidaye took Dot down a shady footpath, moist with ferns and ivy, heavy hedge-tops meeting overhead. At the end, in sunlight, was a large building with high windows and a big main door.

Mrs Hollidaye put her flowers in a tin bucket of water in the porch where other bunches of flowers were being collected.

'Is it a hospital?' said Dot. 'We had the flowers where my baby was.'

'St Michael and All Angels, dear,' said Mrs Hollidaye. 'It's our parish church. Though I dare say, long long ago, sick people probably came here to seek a cure.'

Dot liked the sound of the name, Michael. She wished that Baby had been a Michael. And all angels.

'At Baby's hospital, you could buy a bunch from the flower-lady near the gate. People took them in for them other people what was sick but we didn't never have no dosh.'

Dot wanted to point out that Baby had died anyway but remembered Gloria's warning to mind her P's and Q's.

Inside St Michael and All Angels, women were arranging the flowers in golden tubs. There were tall gleaming candlesticks, a glittering cross so bright it seemed to burn, and an enormous golden eagle with hooked beak and shiny dangerous eye.

'Gold!' whispered Dot. 'I ain't never seen so much real gold before! Bet they ain't got this much even up the palace.'

'No, not gold. Brass. But it's all awfully nicely polished,

49

isn't it? Mrs Buss and Mrs Cheese, that's our two brass ladies, come in and see to it on Fridays. Provided they can get hold of the Brasso. We'll say a little prayer for your baby, shall we?'

Dot didn't know. So she grinned vaguely in a way that could have meant yes or could have meant no. 'He died and all,' she said.

'Yes, my dear, that's why I thought it would be nice to say a little prayer, to remind our dear Lord to take care of him.'

'Them nurses took care of him,' said Dot.

But perhaps they hadn't cared enough? Perhaps our dear Lord would have a better chance.

'Anyway, I think it was a bit our fault, like. See, we used to visit him every day. But then there was that day she gave me the brooch what she said I wasn't never to forget. And we didn't go to see him. That's what done for him.'

'Nonsense, my dear, that's just superstition. He died of pneumonia. There was nothing anyone could have done.'

Mrs Hollidaye took off her leather gloves and laid them neatly on top of her handbag on the pew beside her, straightened her hat and unhooked a cushion which hung from a brass hook beneath the shelf. The cushion was embroidered with a pattern of golden keys. She knelt down on the cushion, placed her ungloved hands together, closed her eyes and appeared to be either thinking or sleeping in an upright kneeling position.

Dot decided she had better copy Mrs Hollidaye. She found a similar cushion hanging in front of her place, sewn in neat wool stitches. Hers had an embroidered picture of a lamb standing in a field of flowers with yellow light sprouting out from around its head. The lamb had a nice expression rather like a kitten's. Dot didn't want to hurt its face so she placed her knees carefully to one side of the lamb so that they pressed into the sewn field of flowers on the edge.

Dot closed her eyes. She could see nothing except a vivid scarlet blur, the colour of a London bus. So she thought about Baby, not sad thoughts but ordinary ones. She remembered him propped up by the nurses, waving his little hands about. That was before he became too ill even to be propped. She remembered one time when a nurse had beckoned Dot into a side room, pulled over a metal chair for Dot, and brought the bundle to her wrapped in a bulky scratchy blanket. She had laid him in Dot's arms and let her hold him on her own.

Even though he was small, he'd felt heavy. He had seemed to be sleeping, yet even in sleep his closed eyelids quivered and his tiny fists were half-clenched. When he woke he gazed up at Dot almost as though he knew her, yet she couldn't be sure if he really saw her, for his eyes had a distant faraway look like a sailor in the Navy staring across the Pacific seas.

After that, the other nurses always made her wait in the corridor. Perhaps they'd known all along what was going to happen to him. Perhaps they hadn't wanted her to see.

Dot opened her eyes to glance sideways at Mrs Hollidaye but she was still in the same position, kneeling, so Dot lowered her lids and, though she hadn't meant to she found herself thinking about Gloria, still asleep in that high bed with the soft eiderdown. Poor Gloria who hadn't had breakfast. No cooked egg inside its shell and served on a plate patterned with a picture of cauliflowers, no rich fruit lying in sweet juice, no butter, no bread, no yellow cream. And no coming to this gold place to see the green and multi-coloured flowers.

When Mrs Hollidaye had finished her praying and they were leaving the church, she stopped at the back and showed Dot a book with writing in it.

'It's very sad when a baby dies,' she said. 'But at least when they are so very young, they have no chance to sin and bring more wickedness into this world. Well, that's how I comforted myself. We could put your little brother's name in here. It's our parish record of who is specially in need of prayer each week. The sick and the departed. What was his name?'

Dot found to her surprise that, just as she often could no longer remember what her father's face looked like, now she couldn't remember Baby's name. How could it go so quickly?

She said, 'He didn't have no name. He did have something official because the nurses, like, said he had to. That's the law, they said. But me Mum weren't there, so them nurses had to invent it themselves. Anything they could think of.'

'I expect they wanted to make sure he was baptized,' said Mrs Hollidaye.

'Me and Gloria, we always called him Baby.'

'"Baby". That's lovely.' Mrs Hollidaye handed the pen to Dot. 'Would you like to write it?' She pointed to the place on the open page of the book. Dot thought it was the loveliest book she'd ever seen. Around the edge of each page, was a pattern of angels' heads with blue wings. St Michael and All Angels. It would have been nice if Baby's name could have been Michael.

Dot shook her head. 'Can't do writing,' she said.

'Very well. I'll do it.'

'Can you write his name "Michael" as well as "Baby". I just remembered. I think that was his name what the nurses give him.' She knew that writing his name was never going to get him back, even if they wrote it hundreds of times in the most beautiful book in the world. But she liked Mrs Hollidaye. She didn't want to upset her.

'So me and Gloria, we won't be seeing Baby no more,' Dot said firmly.

'That's right, my dear. He's in heaven now. Quite safe for always. Better than being sad and sick.'

'He weren't sad,' Dot said, though she liked the sound of 'quite safe for always'. She'd have liked that for herself and Gloria. It sounded better than burning in those fires of hell that Mrs Parvis once mentioned.

'We had better be on our way to pick up Mrs Squirrel now.'

On their way across the churchyard Mrs Hollidaye

pointed down to something on the ground. 'That's my baby, there,' she said. 'Oh, yes, I had some fine sons. But this one was my little girl. She lived six hours. Such a fleeting while.'

Dot looked down and saw only the tussocky grass and a flat square stone.

'There's writing on it,' she said, touching the letters carved in the stone. 'What's it say?'

'Rose Davenport Hollidaye. Underneath it says when she was born. And then, *Gone to be with Jesus.*'

'Rose,' said Dot. 'That's nice. Like a flower. Gloria give me my name like one of them stars. My Mum lives for the films. Dorothy Lamour. She been writ up in all the cinemas. But I ain't writ up nowhere. It's good having it writ up like that. Then you can't forget. Our Baby ain't got one of these. Wish he had though. See, where we live up London, there ain't no grass or garden places you could do this.'

'They have graveyards in London too. People have to be buried in consecrated ground.'

'Don't think so,' said Dot. 'Not round about where we live.'

She knew where London people were buried. Under rubble in bomb-sites and they didn't get any nice flat stone with writing either. They just got a wooden notice saying LOOTERS WILL BE SHOT.

53

10   The End of an Afternoon

At lunchtime Dot's ears began hurting inside her head as though they were filling with hot fire. She found she still couldn't eat. Mrs Hollidaye didn't force her. Dot wondered about the apple tree growing from a pip. Perhaps it was the branches that were spiking inside her ears, grating against the back of her throat?

Afterwards, while Loopy Lil cleared the meal, Mrs Hollidaye put on her galoshes and took Dot round the walled kitchen garden.

'To show you something my dear, very special. And well worth the waiting for. Till you're really hungry.'

She bent down to lift a domed glass lid lying on a heap of earth. Green leaves and curling tendrils were escaping under the edge of the dome like curly hair from beneath a helmet.

'Take a peek under the cloche, my dear. And you'll see my babies.'

Snuggled in the mass of leaves lay five growing objects, round and green, streaked with yellow. And there was that strange smell again which Dot recognized from the darkness of the night before of things dying and rotting and growing again. Now, in daylight, she knew it was not something to fear.

'There's my little dears,' said Mrs Hollidaye, speaking to the fruits. 'Melons. And coming along nicely. Just like children. All they need is a warm corner, a nice bit of sun, careful feeding—that's splendid pig manure we put in— and plenty of interest. Then they grow and grow. Ooh, they *are* going to be such a treat! So long as the frost doesn't get to them first. Or the mice. If the frost comes early, I'll just have to bring them into the airing cupboard, won't I?'

Dot wondered what melon tasted like. It looked so green and hard.

'Sweet and juicy when they're at perfection. The nearest taste to heaven, I'd say,' said Mrs Hollidaye. 'Though perhaps not quite as good as the banana.'

Dot wished she'd never made that claim about eating bananas.

'D'you know, the first time I tasted melon wasn't till I was well over twenty? A long time ago. I went on a tour with my sisters to see the frescoes in Florence. At our *pensione*, they gave us melon every day! A whole one each with the top cut off. And what a lovely time that was. With all those beautiful paintings to see. Italy's a really wonderful country, I wonder if I'll ever get a chance to go back.'

'Italy!' said Dot with surprise. 'But them's enemy!'

Perhaps down here in the countryside the people hadn't ever known who the enemy was. Perhaps they didn't know that several of the wickedest men had escaped from Germany and were even now pretending to be other people.

Yet in spite of her unusual ideas about Germans and other foreigners, Dot felt that Mrs Hollidaye was a reliable person. You could talk to her knowing she wouldn't twist what you said like Mrs Parvis, nor fail to understand what you meant like Gloria.

Dot said, 'There was a raid in the night, weren't there?'

'A *raid*? Last night?'

'I heard it. Exploding and that.'

'Oh, that! Why, you poor dear!'

'I woke up. There weren't no siren. But I heard explodings and that. I knew it'd all started up again.'

'No, it was the men clearing the marshes. To make it safe. Though goodness knows why they think they have to do it so early in the morning. Oh, dear, I should've warned you, so you wouldn't be alarmed.'

'I weren't afraid.'

'Sound does travel a long way, doesn't it? It must be

seven miles off. It's these unexploded shells, quite a number littered about and we haven't been allowed down there for so long, it's all barbed wire, I believe. There used to be such wonderful blackberries! Maybe they'll finish soon and we can go blackberrying. It *would* be fun, wouldn't it, with a picnic?'

There were so many new things, blackberrying, tasting melon, a picnic, all waiting to be done. And Baby was never going to get to know about any of them.

'The planes used to drop them off over the marshes.'

Dot realized she meant the bombs not the blackberries.

'Sometimes on their way in to London. Sometimes on their way back. People said it was because they weren't any good at finding their way. That's rubbish of course. They had maps. And the Germans have always been excellent at map-reading. No, I believe those nice young men up there did it on purpose. They didn't *want* to go and kill a lot of people they didn't know. So they looked for somewhere else. Like our marshes. Though I do believe a cow once was maimed. Anyway, the farmer claimed the war damage. And a woman died. Though that wasn't a bomb. Drowned herself in a dyke, poor soul. Unhinged in her mind when her fiancé went down with the *Wessex*, poor dear.'

When Mrs Hollidaye said that she and Miss Lilian had to walk over to fetch the milk from the home farm, she suggested that Dot should stay and rest by the fire. But Dot said she wanted to come too.

'My dear, you are looking too tired. We simply can't use the Ford again today. Because if Mr Bodger found out, that's our warden, he'd be so upset. I gave his wife some mulberries last autumn and I know he trusts us with the petrol allowance and anyway this beastly rationing should be over soon, so I know I shouldn't complain when some people have had it much worse up in town. My dear! I've an idea! We'll harness the goat. Wouldn't that be splendid, Miss Lilian? Then, Dorothy, you can ride in the cart.'

When the goat was made ready, Loopy Lil helped Dot up onto the little red-painted cart with the empty milk cans clattering on the wooden seat beside her, while Mrs Hollidaye took the leading-rein at the front.

There were pictures in one of Gloria's magazines of the decorated carriage pulled by plumed horses that Her Majesty had travelled in before she became Her Majesty the Queen, when she was still just a Lady, on her way to be married. Dot thought how it had probably felt like this, jolting yet stately.

Then she thought of the blackberrying and the melon, of the feathered hens that laid eggs, and of the church eagle of glinting metal that glowed like gold. She was finding out many new things that Baby would never know of.

'Would you say,' Dot asked, 'it's more like London, or more like round about here?'

'Where, dear?'

'At heaven.'

The goat stopped abruptly and tried to chew at the hem of Mrs Hollidaye's brown jacket.

'You know, my dear, the gospels are not at *all* clear on that point. Personally I would like to believe it to be peacefully verdant. As it says so clearly in the Psalms. Walking in green pastures. Beside still waters.'

Dot did not know what Psalms were, but she felt she was beginning to understand about quiet and gentle greenness because she saw it all around her. This seemed to be a place where, despite noises in the night and a few dangers like trees that grew inside you and made your throat choke, a person might feel safe for always.

The goat suddenly trotted eagerly forward and Mrs Hollidaye had to run to keep hold of the leather strap. They passed down the lane between high hedges.

Dot said, 'That's all right, then. I'm glad he's at a nice place like this.'

Better than burning in Mrs Parvis's hot red fires of hell.

The goat stopped again and leaned over to take a bite of springy grass beside the road.

'I think *he's* gone there too,' said Dot.

'What, dear?'

'Him. My old man.'

'Derek? Not to heaven, dear!'

So he *had* gone to that other place where, so Mrs Parvis said, red and orange fires burned day and night, so hot that glass and brick and even solid rock melted to liquid.

'Gloria and me went to see him once,' said Dot. 'I don't reckon he's there no more. She don't talk about it. We had to go on the Green Line bus.'

It had been a long ride to an enclosure full of low single-storeyed huts of corrugated iron with cinder paths around, and all set in a large flat field of sparse greying grass.

'It was military, Gloria said. She was blinking right. There was soldiers everywhere. They was at the gate, so we couldn't go in. Gloria had to show this special letter what she had about him before they'd even look at us.'

Dot wasn't used to talking so much about her father. Usually Gloria told her to shut her trap. Mrs Hollidaye didn't.

Some of the men inside the hut had peered out like timid ghosts. She hadn't seen what her father looked like. He hadn't come out and she hadn't been allowed in. Gloria had gone in and a person at a window had waved once but Dot hadn't known if it was him. She'd sat on the stubby grass, cut short as the back of a soldier's head.

Afterwards, Gloria had said, 'That grass were clipped flat so there weren't nowhere for a running man to hide.'

They reached the big white gate at the entrance to Mrs Hollidaye's driveway. The goat twisted its neck to make a grab at a fallen twig on the ground.

'No one never comes back from there, do they?' Dot said.

'From heaven, dear? No, I'm afraid you won't see the baby again. Not till you reach heaven. But you never know, maybe your mother will be able to have another one later.'

Dot hadn't meant where Baby was. She knew she'd never see *him* again. She meant that place where her father was, wherever that was. She'd begun to guess he was probably dead too and they'd forgotten to tell her, just like nobody told her straight when Baby died.

She was glad. She didn't ever want to have to see him.

Gloria came down, bright and freshly lipsticked, in time for tea. They were in the glass-roofed, glass-sided room which Mrs Hollidaye called the conservatory. The conservatory was warm, light and moist, filled with growing plants in pots. Through the glass and the vines overhead could be seen the blue sky and the white clouds, so that it was like being both indoors and out at the same time.

At teatime, there was honey, sour-milk scones and plum jam where you had to mind out for the stones. The bread and butter was served not in huge chunks like at elevenses, but on a pretty dish with a golden edge, in thinly-cut slices.

Gloria was hungry.

'I'm telling you,' she said, 'when I heard that big clock in the hall striking the five, you could've knocked me down with a feather! Seems like I been dead to the world for weeks! I'm telling you, Mrs Hollidaye, you'll get plenty of work out of me tomorrow. Anything you need doing around the place. And that's a promise. Come on, pet, put that where the flies won't get it.' She urged Dot to drink a glassful of fresh milk. 'Does you good, that does. Oh well, please yourself, ducky. Me and Lil, at least we know how to trough up good and proper, don't we, Lil?'

Loopy Lil, with plum jam already streaked like blood round her mouth, grinned cheerfully and went on tucking in.

By the end of that first day, Dot knew, despite her throbbing head, her painful neck and throat, that this was a good place. She didn't mind how long they had to stay. She wouldn't even mind if Gloria went away and left her.

Loopy Lil began piling the tea-things on to the tray to carry back to the kitchen, and Mrs Hollidaye suggested Gloria should go and help bring in the vegetables from the shed for supper, when an insistent bell began ringing out somewhere within the house. It clanged urgently, like a fire-engine dashing towards a disaster, like the ambulance thundering along behind to retrieve the bodies. It would not stop.

'Oh, bother!' said Mrs Hollidaye, calmly putting another teacup on the tray, not at all upset by the persistent clamour. 'Telephone. It's Nurse River, I'll be bound, someone needs to be driven somewhere. And I did so want to dig up a few artichokes this evening. Jerusalem artichokes, they make a lovely cream soup so long as you don't mind the flatulence.'

The telephone was in her hall.

Mrs Hollidaye got up and went to it. Then Gloria was called. After that, everything changed and everything that had seemed to Dot to be all right disappeared. Just when she thought they'd got away from it, change and disruption had caught up with them again.

Dot sat rigid and shivering on the wicker armchair in the conservatory. Loopy Lil went on piling more and more things haphazardly on to the tray.

11 In the Hen-house

Dot could hear them just inside the house. Mrs Hollidaye was doing most of the speaking.

'Yes, my dear, I do understand how it must seem hard to you.'

Dot knew it was something to do with her father.

'But you've got to try. For yourself. For the child. For him too.'

And Dot knew that Gloria was crying.

'My dear, he's going to need you more than ever before.'

Dot could hear Gloria saying she wouldn't and she couldn't.

Then Mrs Hollidaye said, 'My dear girl, you have to start making a home. And you know that you will always be welcome back here on another occasion. Now, while you go and dry those eyes, I'll look up the trains.'

Dot in the conservatory watched as Loopy Lil slowly tried to pick up the unsteady tray of china. Dot knew what was going to happen.

The wobbling teacup on the top fell first, the rest followed. Cups, saucers, teapot, milk jug with its little muslin cloth, plates and splattered jam. The crashing seemed to go on forever as tiny broken fragments bounced with a dainty tinkle across the brick floor.

Loopy Lil stared round at the destruction with a look of hopelessness as though she did not understand how it had happened. Dot knew that Mrs Hollidaye would come to comfort her, to reassure her that it wasn't her fault. Poor Loopy Lil, she had a screw loose. She'd only been trying to help.

But Dot couldn't do anything for her because she had to

escape. She must hide before Gloria found her. She darted for the open doors and down the stone step to the garden. She ran round the outside of the house, barging past bushes and shrubs. She found her way to the kitchen. She wanted to go along the side passage and up the back stairs to the bedroom with the toys where she could safely hide.

But the house was too big and she lost her way. Instead, she was in a dark lobby full of musty boots. She ran out again through a side entrance. She recognized where she was. This was the yard where Mrs Hollidaye fed the hens, throwing down the corn for them to peck up.

She could hear Gloria behind calling for her.

She ran back across the yard to the hen-house, through the netting gate, across the muddy enclosure, scattering hens at each step. Then crouching low, she squeezed herself through the hens' low archway, and into the dark warm gloom of their hut. More hens sat clucking on their roosts.

The hens were all right. They didn't have to go anywhere. This was their home and they could stay here always.

'Going time, Dot,' said Gloria outside. 'Come on out.'

Dot kept still and quiet, head down and hunched like a bird sleeping, hoping Gloria wouldn't know she was in there. But the fowl were irritated by this invasion of their hut and their clucking gave her away.

'Come on, pet. We know you're in there.'

'We only just got here!' Dot yelled, not coming out. 'Where we going, anyway?'

'Home now, duckypet. Got to catch the train. Last one leaves at twenty-past.'

'No!' said Dot, though she knew she'd have to do what Gloria wanted, go where Gloria went.

'Not coming!' she shouted in the dusty gloom. 'Going to stay here.' And when she heard Gloria outside rattling the hen-house door, she screamed it again and again till Gloria managed to get the latch undone and came in and dragged her yelling through the droppings and feathers and washed her face under the water pump and dried it on her hanky.

Mrs Hollidaye was there too, and more gently than Gloria asked, 'Were there any more eggs in there, did you notice? I collected earlier. But sometimes there's an extra egg or two. Come, we must choose some for you to take back with you. The speckledy brown ones are best.'

Mrs Hollidaye found Gloria a blue suitcase with proper metal clips to pack their things in. 'It's a spare. I shan't be going anywhere for a while. You can bring it back next time you come. Then you can use your paper carriers for these, can't you?'

She gave Gloria two jars of jam, and six fresh eggs packed in a special cardboard box with separate soft spaces to keep each one safe. She gave Gloria money so that she wouldn't have to pretend Dot was a babe-in-arms.

On the train ride home, the compartment no longer seemed like a compact travelling home. It was just a train with lumpy seats and smuts. Dot sat hunched in her corner, Gloria in another, each far from the other.

Eventually Dot asked, 'Was he a brave man?'

'Reverend Hollidaye? I'll say, I told you about him.'

'No, I mean *him*. The other one.'

'Who's that?'

'Him. My father, was he like some kind of hero?'

'Your old man a hero? Don't make me laugh! Your Dad couldn't have knocked the skin off a rice pudding.'

Dot tried not to look at Gloria's face. Why would anyone want to go and see a man who was a coward?

Dot remembered one of the things she'd overheard Mrs Hollidaye telling Gloria just before Loopy Lil crashed the tray. 'You know, my dear, love's a funny thing. If you want it, you'll find it can grow in the most unexpected places.'

Dot hadn't known what it meant. It made her think of green melons growing under glass lids. That was an unexpected place. Perhaps it could also mean loving a man who wasn't there and didn't deserve to be loved.

Dot thought about that place where they'd visited him long ago, with soldiers guarding the main gate, and long low buildings surrounded by grass clipped so flat there was nowhere for a running man to hide. Then she thought about those other long low huts she'd seen in the fenced-off meadow beyond St Michael and All Angels. Mrs Hollidaye said that's where the prisoners of war were housed. The buildings were the same kind as where her faceless father had been.

It was a tiny hope. But if he was a war prisoner, soon they'd be sending him back. That's what Mrs Hollidaye said was happening.

'Repatriation. It's a slow old business, putting everybody in the country they started from. But in the end they should all be home with their mothers. Poor boys. That's where they belong. Or with their sisters, or their sweethearts.'

If he was one of *them*, that's why they were hurrying back to London, so Gloria could say goodbye before he was put on a ship and Dot wouldn't ever have to see him again.

The train rumbled through the dark. Dot tried again.

'Is he one of them foreigners, then?'

'Foreigners? How d'you mean?'

'I saw some where we just been. In the big kitchen. They was working in the fields. But they gonna get took home soon.'

'Them's prisoners of war.'

'I know. Germans. Is my old man one of them?'

'What kind of thing to say is that!' said Gloria. 'All that good food you been getting, it's gone to your head, I'd say. In fact I'm darn sure it has, the way you behaved. What made you want to crawl in with them mucky birds like that? I've never been so ashamed in my life. You don't get that kind of behaviour from me.'

'I just wanted to know about him,' said Dot, crying now because she had made Gloria angry. 'Sorry, honest. Won't never say it again.'

As the train drew into Victoria Station, Gloria softened. 'There, there. Don't take on so.'

She crossed over to sit beside Dot. She put her arm round her.

64

'Come now, pet, let's kiss and make up and I'll tell you about him. Biggin Hill, I met him, Empire Air Day. Oh, he was beautiful. In them days we could really go for a man in uniform. We was married real quick. Well in them days you never knew what might happen next. Then you come along not so long after.'

She gave Dot a peck on the cheek.

'Oh, my, you're warm as toast, aren't you? You took a chill? Ooh, ducky, I do hope you haven't gone and caught something nasty from them birds.'

12 Bad Germs

'So you're back, then!' said Mrs Parvis.

She didn't seem too pleased even when Gloria gave her both pots of jam. 'So you wasn't gone away long, the pair of you, was you?'

Dot tugged at Gloria's sleeve. She wanted to get in off the doorstep. She wanted to lie down.

'A nervy little thing, isn't she? Fat lot of good the countryside done *her*. Couldn't you have left her down there with that woman friend?'

Gloria began to edge along the hallway.

'So you got the message all right? About hubby, was it? Anything to oblige. Though you know being telegraph-boy isn't in my normal line of business. Still, I said to myself, so she *has* got a husband after all, because I was beginning to put two and two together and ask myself a few questions. We keep a respectable house here as well you know. So he's being demobbed at last, is he?'

'We got some eggs too, Mrs Parvis,' said Gloria. 'Would you like a couple?'

'Ooh ta, ever so. Well I hope you sort yourselves out nice and quick. Because I shan't do with him lodging here long. That's only a single room. At that rent it has to be.'

'Hold your horses, Mrs Parvis. You won't get *him* stopping here, not for all the tea in China. He's fixing us up in a flat, with kitchenette, out Godalming way, a live-in maintenance job.'

Dot knew it was all dreams. She could tell with Gloria. There was the way her lips moved when she was lying.

'Glad to hear it. I was pushing it, letting the child in. So now I've got to be cruel to be kind. Because you know that

66

you won't get on that priority housing list if I'm soft on you.'

Dot preferred Mrs Hollidaye's way of talking, always trying to see the good side of things. Even when it was something bad, like the mice-damage in the apple room, or the wasps' nest in the orchard, or even your husband jumping off a plane and dying, she managed to see the good part of it. Mr Brown was a bit like that too.

Dot said, 'In the country, where we just been, there's this lady where we stayed what hasn't eaten a banana so long she's forgotten the taste, and what's growing these melons in her garden. Under a lid.'

'In the country, in the country. I'm not sure I can stand that kind of talk,' snapped Mrs Parvis. 'If it was all so blooming wonderful, I dunno why your Mum didn't let you stay put.'

That night the air in the basement room became so thick it was like inhaling the black tar they put on the road. Dot knew it must be the enemy had dropped their gas canisters to suffocate women and children in a gas-attack. She saw how the dark room had filled with transparent figures who marched along the walls singing and mocking, who wrapped themselves around her so that she was suffocated in their embrace, then turned to broken bricks and choking mortar dust which cascaded in torrents on to her, flattening her to the bed so that her limbs ached with pain and she couldn't move.

Each breath was fire and splinters of ice. Her throat was filled with coils of barbed wire.

Towards morning she woke limp and exhausted, shivering with cold. As delirium receded, she knew it had all been dreams.

'My throat hurts,' she whispered.

But Gloria wasn't there. Her black hat with the little veil had gone from the shelf, and her best peep-toe shoes. Dot realized she'd already left to visit the man who was a gutless jink.

Dot guessed by the papery men lurking inside the walls that she must be ill. But if so, how had it happened? Was it in some way her own fault? And how ill did you have to be before you died?

She put on her coat and got back into the bed.

During the day it came again, the shadows falling off the walls. And Gloria wouldn't be back for hours. It was a long bus-ride to reach those low huts standing behind the high fence.

Dot got up and went along to the kitchen for Mrs Parvis's High Tea. Two wet floury potatoes were dished on to her plate but she couldn't eat them. Mrs Parvis scraped them back into the pot.

'Waste not, want not,' she said with a frown of disapproval.

The table lurched up at Dot.

'That child don't look any too well, do she?' she heard Mrs Parvis's voice, far away at the end of the table. 'Say, Dotty, you all right?'

Dot's throat was so swollen she couldn't speak. She wanted to drink. As she held the cup of tea to her mouth, she felt herself tumble down into a deep well.

She began sliding from the chair towards the gaping hole in the floor. There was nothing she could do to save herself. She tried to remember what Mrs Hollidaye had said about the many different ways of being brave. She clutched at the slithery sides but there was no grip.

Way up above in the light at the top of the well Mrs Parvis was speaking but Dot knew it was nothing to do with her.

'Said I'd keep an eye on the kiddy for an hour or two. Now look what's happened! It's a disgrace.'

'It's hardly her fault if the child falls ill,' said one of the lodgers.

'That's as maybe. But I can't go having my place turned into a fever ward. All them germs. Where'll that lead us? Before we know where we are we'll all be down with it like flies. As if I don't have enough on my plate already.'

Dot felt herself gathered up from the kitchen floor and Mr Brown's face came into view, kindly and familiar. She reached out for his hand. Benign Mr Brown.

'Now, then,' said Mrs Parvis sternly and pushed Mr Brown out of the way. 'That'll be all for now, Mr Brown. Everything under control and we can manage on our own.'

When she was laid on the bed Dot felt the room spin.

'Did you ever play cloud pictures?' Mrs Hollidaye had asked when they went over the fields to fetch the creamy milk from Home Farm.

'Don't know,' said Dot and wondered if it was anything like princesses.

Mrs Hollidaye explained. 'We have to lie down on our backs. Springy moss is best, here on this bank. We look up into the sky, we watch the shapes of the clouds changing till we recognize a picture. Do you see, my dear, up there now? A clown with a laughing face?'

Dot looked upwards and saw the smiling clown.

'And now he's changing into a little dog, d'you see, my dear?'

Dot saw the little dog too, dancing. Then it was her turn.

'I can see fire,' she had said. 'Flames.' She saw them swirling and licking across the sky burning up everything. She pointed them out to Mrs Hollidaye.

Dot tried to find beautiful pictures like Mrs Hollidaye did, of meadow flowers, and laughing children, cathedrals and fairy coaches.

A long time later, or perhaps only a few seconds, she thought she saw her father's face white as paper, floating among the clouds, then it dissolved into the face of an elderly stranger bending over her. If only Gloria was here. He wrapped her in a scarlet blanket, and carried her up the outside area steps. It was already dark outside. The ambulance stood in the road.

'Gloria!' Dot croaked. She knew she shouldn't cause trouble to people. Mrs Parvis was always telling her so. She wanted to cry.

'That's all right, sunshine,' said the ambulance man. 'We're taking care of you.'

Dot turned to see Mrs Parvis, arms folded akimbo across her floral apron, rigid on her front steps.

They slammed the ambulance doors. The windows were like the windows of the children's ward where Baby used to be, of white glass which you couldn't see through.

One of the lodgers was travelling with her. The woman saw Dot staring and smiled.

'There you are. Everything all right now?'

What on earth was *she* doing in the ambulance? Was she ill too?

At the hospital, in a cold tiled room, they asked questions and wrote down answers.

'Mother's name? Father's name?'

Dot struggled to sit up. 'Airman,' she croaked. 'Dead now.'

'Ssh, dear, don't try to talk,' said the woman lodger, and the nurse made her lie down.

'Has she ever been admitted to this hospital before?'

'Yes,' said Dot, sitting up again. 'Every day. To see Baby.'

But they didn't mean it like that.

Name? Age? Date of birth? Address? Religion? How long ill? Any fever yesterday? Immunized against diptheria? Opened her bowels today? Ever been in contact with any person carrying typhoid? Any family history of rheumatic fever?

After that Dot couldn't be bothered. She let the woman lodger answer since that's what they seemed to want.

After the questions, the woman lodger went away and they took off Dot's clothes and touched and prodded at her neck, her ears and her throat. But she knew she mustn't make a fuss. Finally they wheeled her on a trolley down the draughty brown corridor, through the swing doors, into Ward 3-South where a dim light showed the children lying down.

Dot was put into a bed with high sides. She wanted to explain that she wasn't a baby and didn't need a cot.

'Haven't had no tea,' Dot croaked. 'Didn't get no dinner neither.'

The nurse pulled up the metal sides and closed them

with a clang so that Dot was like a caged prisoner. 'It's too late for that now,' said the nurse. 'You'll have to wait for morning. You'll find that comes soon enough.'

A child in a bed nearby began to whimper and Dot wondered if not crying when you wanted to counted as being brave.

Later that night one of Dot's teeth came out. She thought at first that it was an apple pip in her mouth. She touched the jellied space in her mouth and found a drop of blood like a shiny ladybird resting on her finger.

She felt with her tongue. Other teeth moved freely in a way that they had never moved before. She was breaking into pieces. Maybe more teeth would come out. Maybe her arms, then her legs, her hair, her arms, her fingers, her thumbs till there would be nothing left of her for Gloria to find.

She called out to the night-nurse who scurried over when she saw the red smear on the stiff white pillowcase. But as soon as she saw the tooth, she lost interest.

'Is that all it was?' she said. 'Thought you were bleeding to death? Thought the sky was falling in on your head? Ssh now, and go back to sleep. Or d'you want the whole ward to wake up just for one milk tooth?'

13   Ward 3-South

When Baby had been here, Dot remembered how she had yearned to be with him, amongst those quiet children so calm in their tidy beds. But the ward was no longer shining with peaceful light. What had appeared then to be contentment turned out now to be cold loneliness. And once in, there was no way through the blank windows.

It came and went in swirling waves that rushed down from the ceiling and swallowed her up. She forgot who she was, how long she had been here.

They told her she was lucky, but Dot couldn't understand how.

Four times a day the nurse came towards her across the wide spaces of lino with the shiny basin containing the rattling metal syringe. Four times a day, the nurse pulled back the white cover, turned Dot on her side, pulled up the gown and thrust the needle in with the savage pain of a bayonet.

The first time, Dot cried out at this new kind of hurt. Later she knew not to make any sound, otherwise the nurse said, 'Don't you *want* to get better?' Then she told Dot, 'You're a lucky little scallywag! Ten years ago and you'd have died!'

Sometimes she saw nurses whispering about her and wanted to hide.

When Gloria came, pattering across the ward in all her best, Dot couldn't bear to see her pretty face and turned away on the pillow with shut eyes.

Why did you let them bring me here? What have I done? she wanted to say. When can I get out?

Each bed had a locker beside it. On top of some were

displayed heavy glass bottles of fizzy pop, or coloured post-cards, or jig-saws or ragdolls with floppy arms. Dot didn't mind about the toys and she knew she couldn't ask for ginger pop because that cost money but she would have liked to have had her victory token back. Gloria had told her she'd got to keep it for ever. It had been in her coat pocket when they took her clothes away. Now it was gone for ever.

Dot managed to attract the attention of the girl lying in the next bed.

'Want to play a game? Film stars?'

The sick girl nodded.

'You start, then,' said Dot.

But the girl didn't know how to play and Dot hadn't enough voice to explain. By the time she had, they'd moved the girl away to another ward. Dot didn't see her again.

Gloria came every day, just as she had for Baby.

'Mustn't stay long,' she said, giving Dot's hand a little squeeze. 'I've started this little job see, pet. Ooh, your hand, it ain't half skinny. I'll have to call you spindle-shanks if you let yourself get any thinner!'

She was usherette at the Essoldo cinema, showing people to their seats. 'Matinées only. I get to see all the films. Well, it helps pass the time. I'm saving a bit up for when your old man gets home. *To Have and Have Not*, that's showing now. Ooh, it's a lovely one!'

Gloria's lipstick was brighter than ever, and she had a fitted red two-piece with *Essoldo* embroidered in cream on the top pocket.

'Being a good girl, aren't you, ducky? Saying please and thank you? Don't want to hear no tales told about you from them nice nurses. You eat up your dinners, too.'

Where her tooth had fallen out a sturdy new one was forcing its way up, with frilled edges and ridged from top to bottom. Dot asked Gloria for the powder compact she kept in her bag. When she looked in the little round mirror, she saw that she wasn't falling to pieces. She was turning into a different person with a different face.

After Gloria had gone, lying in her cot with nothing to do, nothing to look at, Dot told herself about the hens laying in the country. She went into the hen-house and looked at their eggs. She thought she saw the Germans still working in the fields, and now they were picking up potatoes from the muddy ground. But perhaps she'd never really been there at all. Perhaps she'd just imagined it, like she'd imagined the pallid papery men buried in the walls.

Since she no longer had her own victory brooch to hold, she thought about Mrs Hollidaye's, pinned to the lapel of her hairy jacket. Its design, like Dot's, was of crossed flags but wasn't made of scratchy tin with rusting edges. Hers was shiny jewels, blue, red and diamond bright which twinkled when they caught the light.

'Gloria said you was ever so posh, bit like our king and queen. You don't look that posh. Except you got them jewels. I ain't never seen jewels like that before.'

'Yes, they are rather grand, aren't they, my dear? The red duster, the white ensign and the Union Jack.' Mrs Hollidaye glanced down at her brooch and touched it like Dot used to touch her token. 'My sons gave it to me. And d'you know, I've worn it every day since. It helps me think of them.'

'I knew Gloria got it wrong. I never thought you was that posh. You ain't got no servants.'

'Well, my dear, we can all be servants, one to another, depending on the need, can't we?'

What strange things she said. But now, lying in a cot while a nurse washed her all over and patted her dry, she saw what Mrs Hollidaye might have meant.

A brown paper parcel arrived by special delivery. The other children on the ward didn't get parcels by post.

'It's for that little slip of a thing at the end.'

A nurse sat on Dot's bed and unwrapped it and Dot knew it was from Mrs Hollidaye.

'What in lawks name is this!' said the nurse holding it up.

Dot wanted to say, 'It's one of Mrs Hollidaye's babies!' but because of her throat, the words stuck like plum stones.

Instead, she managed to croak, 'Eat it. Vegetable.' Or had it been a fruit?

The melon was boiled and brought to Dot next dinner time with her chicken broth all around like a shattered building surrounded by deep trenches full of murky rainwater. Mrs Hollidaye hadn't said anything about cooking it. Slice the top off, scoop out the seeds, and a drop of *Oporto* is what she'd said.

The doctors gathered round her bed. They measured Dot's legs with wooden measuring sticks, and they prodded her ribs while a nurse stood by and held her hand. They didn't usually speak to her, only about her.

They told Gloria, 'This child is malnourished. She has anaemia and first stage rickets.'

An old man in a dark suit with a light strapped round his forehead like a rescue worker's lamp came next and pushed wooden sticks down Dot's throat.

He told Gloria, 'The sooner we get them out the better. But she's got to be A1. So we're sending her home to fatten up. Liver, spinach, cheese, green leaf vegetables.'

'They want to do an operation, pet,' Gloria explained at visiting time. 'Make you fighting fit again. Get rid of them nasty things down your throat what's harbouring the germs. When you're asleep.'

When Dot was asleep was when the dreams came with limbless, fingerless, thumbless, faceless men marching through her head. She didn't want them to do anything then. They must do things when she was awake.

'They can't do that, ducky. That's not how the doctors like it. It would hurt you too much. You have to be asleep.'

Gloria brought some clothes in a carrier. But Dot had changed and so had the skirt and cardigan. They hung strangely, too loose, yet too short as well. Her wrists stuck out. Her legs were bare to way above her knees and her legs felt cold and so thin they'd hardly support her weight. She had to clutch on to Gloria's arm.

'Here, put this on too,' said Gloria. It was a pixie bonnet. 'One of them nice ladies at Mrs P's, middle floor, knitted it up. Said I was to take extra care to keep your ears warm, specially with this wind. Unravelled one of her own woollies specially.' It was a mixture of strange colours and the knitted ties felt scratchy where Gloria knotted them under Dot's chin. 'You'll have to say thank you.'

At first, Mrs Parvis pretended to be pleased to see Dot.

'Oh my! And hasn't she grown tall! So that's what lying in bed all day does for you. I should try it myself if only I had the time.'

But to Gloria she said, 'She's all skin and bone. If you looked at her sideways, you wouldn't never see her at all.'

After that, everything was just the same with Mrs Parvis still complaining as much as ever.

'They gave us that big build-up. The new Britain, that's what our boys been fighting for. Work for all, health for all, that's what they promised.'

'And a good home for everybody,' Gloria agreed. Mrs Parvis glared at her and carried on.

'And now look at us! Right back where we was. Noses to the grindstone. In fact I'd say we're worse off than what we was at the start of it. They can't even tell us what to do with our gas-masks. I'm sick to death of them cluttering up my hall like that. Reminding us of things we don't want to think about.'

The gas-masks hung on their pegs in the narrow hall. Inside each brown case waited the empty skull-face, folded flat, with a flappy rubber nose and hard cylindrical snout, though they frightened Dot less now than they used to.

'At least we never had to wear them,' said Mr Brown quietly. 'We can be thankful for that.'

Dot had worn hers once during a practice. It was smelly inside, made you feel as though you were choking to death and the eye-holes so small you couldn't see out properly.

They'd issued one for Baby too, a gas-bag like a cradle, with a port-hole on the top. It was too cumbersome to hang on a peg in the hall with the others. So Gloria had shoved it out of the way under the bed.

When Gloria went off to the Essoldo, Dot couldn't go

with her. She wasn't allowed in crowded places where there might be germs. She wasn't allowed to get cold. She wasn't allowed to mix with other children.

'They say she's very susceptible,' Gloria explained to Mrs Parvis when she went to borrow an extra shilling for the meter to light the gas fire in the basement room. 'She could catch anything that's around.'

'Mollycoddling,' said Mrs Parvis under her breath. 'That's what it is, she ought to be back in school, a big girl like that. Besides, what if all my lodgers was asking for favours? I'm not a lending bank.'

In the afternoon, when Gloria had left for work, Dot pulled out Baby's gas-mask to look at it again. It was covered in grey dust. Seeing it, and thinking of him safely in heaven with no risk now of being zipped into this airless rubber gas-bag made Dot start to cry. She didn't understand why. She hadn't cried about him before. She sobbed so much that Mrs Parvis heard through the wall and came in and told her off. She made her get into bed and said she was sending for the blue ladies right away.

She must have told Gloria off too, for the very next day, Gloria said, 'You got to go off to the country, ducks, health visitor says. For your convalescence.'

Dot didn't know what her convalescence was.

'To get you in the pink. For your operation. Like the nice man said. We don't want you hopping the twig.'

'I *am* in the pink,' said Dot, though she knew she wasn't or she wouldn't have allowed herself to weep the day before.

'Can't you come too?'

'I dunno, pet. It's dull down there. There ain't nothing for me to do.'

'What if it's all changed and they don't know me no more?'

'Listen, pet, she's said she'll have you. So what more d'you want? Jam on *both* sides? I'll put you in charge of the guard and you'll be as right as rain.'

Dot felt she was an unwanted item of luggage being sent away.

14 Miss Spindle-Shanks

Mrs Hollidaye met Dot at the train with the Ford drawn right up to the station exit.

'My dear, I won't kiss you. Just in case of the germs. We've got to treat you like best bone china. But don't mind the dogs. They're just longing to see you. Dogs have different germs, can't possibly harm you.' She was wearing her felt hat and her tweed jacket with the jewelled brooch pinned to the lapel. Everything was just as it should be.

'I decided I really *must* bring the motor. And if that nosy old constable asks about petrol, I shall tell him it's an emergency. And if he doesn't believe me, well, we shall have to see what we shall see, won't we?'

She bundled Dot on to the front seat with rugs up to the chin. The wool gave off a friendly smell of the dogs who had been lying on it.

'And here's the hot water bottle for your feet, my dear,' said Mrs Hollidaye. 'And there's a flask of tea if you need it. Though we'll be home before you can say Jack Robinson. And Dorothy dear, I must warn you, you're hardly going to *recognize* Miss Lilian! All new teeth! Top and bottom. That's the new welfare. *Do* tell her how nice she looks, won't you? Of course you will. Only she's rather selfconscious at the moment.'

Loopy Lil's new smile of regular gleaming teeth was the only change. Otherwise everything was reassuringly the same. The yapping of the small dogs, the smells of musty dampness, of jam and paraffin, and welcoming wood-smoke, the vase of flowers on a polished table in the hall.

'Now you're not to lift a finger, my dear, is she, Lilian? Until you're quite better.'

'I *am*. I'm fit as a fiddle!' Dot said. 'Skinny as a whipping post, that's what Gloria says, and sound as a roach.'

But the journey in the guard's van like lost luggage had exhausted her, so she didn't protest about going straight up with Loopy Lil, being changed into one of Mrs Hollidaye's pink flannel nightgowns and tucked into a cocoon of pillows with a hot stone bottle wrapped in a worn silk vest at her feet. There was a fire burning in the grate and a china chamber-pot painted with birds and flowers beneath the bed.

Her supper was on a tray, a plate of yellow buttered eggs, pink rhubarb with cream, a glass of milk and a tiny glass vase of flowers.

'I'll put the snowdrops just here,' Mrs Hollidaye said. 'So you can see them. I do like a person who likes flowers. I believe, my dear, that seeing beautiful things around does so help a soul to feel strong, wouldn't you say? The Ministry did tell us not to waste effort growing flowers, but somehow one always felt they were not quite as right as they might have been on that one. Now you've found the chamber haven't you, under the bed, so you won't have to go far in the night.'

Mrs Hollidaye and Loopy Lil settled on either side of the bedroom fire with the dogs on the carpet between them. Loopy Lil gently smiled her new even welfare smile while Mrs Hollidaye darned lisle stockings.

The wind was getting up, rattling against the wooden shutters, and forcing twigs to scratch against the window panes.

'My dear, aren't we *glad* we're not on the high seas *tonight*!' said Mrs Hollidaye. 'Just think of those poor brave souls out there.'

Dot knew that she had everything she used so much to long for. If only she could will herself strong as a roach. But her legs hurt. So did her neck. A single spoonful of buttered eggs made her feel sick. The clotted cream on the rhubarb had curdled. Her disappointment turned to tears which dripped into the congealing eggs.

Mrs Hollidaye heard the sniffing. 'My dear,' she said, 'limited grey matter Miss Lilian may have, yet still she rejoices to be alive. Sore eyes I may have, but at least I am not blind and can still darn my own stockings. Aching head you may have, but at least you have a head to have aches in.'

She put aside her darning basket, and picked up a book whose dark blue cover was patterned with gold leaves.

'In addition, my dear, you still have ears for listening, I trust?'

She began to read aloud.

Dot saw how the gold patterns on the cover caught the flicker from the fire and flared like Very lights. Mrs Hollidaye's voice was comforting as it rose and fell like the wind. By listening to the story, Dot found she had become brave.

On the breakfast tray the next day, was a different flower, a single brilliant pink blossom with dark leaves so glossy they seemed to have been polished.

'A camellia, my dear. D'you know, the tree hasn't flowered properly for six years. Now it's *such* a sight! Pink all over like an apple tree in May! They seem to shine out like lamps, specially on these grey days. I do wish you could come out and see. Maybe soon. In fact, my dear, we've looked out the old bath chair. From the back of the stables. Lilian's given it a really good dusting down. We've oiled the wheels. And just as soon as you feel up to it, we'll be taking you round the garden for some good lungfuls of God's air.'

Meanwhile, Mrs Hollidaye revealed to Dot how many things were to be done without even having to move from bed. She hung a piece of mutton fat threaded on to string across the window for the blue tits. She showed where Dot must watch across the ragged grass for when the fox came slinking through the bracken towards the hen-house.

She had shown Dot before how to find pictures in the clouds. Now she pointed out how there were pictures in the trees.

The twigs of the beeches drew black pencil lines against the sky in which were hiding animals, and flowers, faces and places. When the breeze rustled the branches, the pictures changed.

With a reel of linen thread and a hooked needle, Mrs Hollidaye showed how to work a crochet collar. With two needles and a ball of wool, she showed how to knit. She gave her books to look at and explained how the printed letters beneath each picture made words which summarized the illustration. She gave her paper and coloured crayons and showed her how she could draw. She taught her how to write her name, how to put the paper in an envelope to be posted to Gloria.

'That's it, my dear. And she'll be so pleased to have it. And put the X's along the bottom and that tells her that you love her and you're thinking of her.'

Dot hadn't been thinking of her. If she thought about Gloria, then she'd have to start thinking about him too. It was better that she thought of neither.

One evening Mrs Hollidaye brought to the bedroom a long wooden box.

'A companion for you, my dear,' she said sliding back the lid. 'I had her when I was a girl.'

In the box under layers of tissue paper lay a doll which Mrs Hollidaye lifted out and placed in Dot's arms. It had long white skirts.

'Ooh, it's beautiful! I ain't never played with a proper doll before. I had some paper dolls one time, but me landlady got rid of them, said they were messing the place up.'

'She's rather old, so one has to be frightfully careful, but I know you will be. She's made from wax. Just the face and hands.' Beneath the long lacy petticoats was a stuffed cotton body wearing a lace camisole.

'I was given two, and I was told by my nurse never to let them near the fire or they'd melt. Oh, what a naughty child I was! I wanted to see if it was true. So I placed one of them up against the fender, to see what would happen. And then

81

her poor face melted like a candle into nothing and how I cried at what I had done to make her lose all her features.'

Dot looked at the doll and thought of its lost companion with a face of dripping wax. Melting cheeks and disappearing noses was what had happened to brave airmen when they caught fire. Their skin burned, their features dissolved and they were left faceless. Gloria met men like that at the airmen's social club.

Dot hugged this doll whose face was still whole. She said, 'It's ever so real-looking, like a person, except it's so titchy.'

Baby had looked like this doll, as though nearly real, yet not quite, with a waxy pale skin, yellow-tinged, bright glassy eyes and a dainty pink mouth. She remembered how she hadn't been allowed to hold him for more than a moment before he had to go back behind the bars of his crib.

'Don't sleep with her, my dear, will you, for though she would not melt, she would crack if she fell. Real mothers don't sleep with their babies. They might overlay them. There was a village woman overlaid her baby last summer, such a terrible thing for everyone. Nurse Willow had already warned her to put it in the crib.'

Dot wondered, did Baby now look like this doll's melted companion, face and hands gone, only his white clothes left?

'When it's time to sleep, why not set her here on the chair to watch over you?' Mrs Hollidaye propped the doll on the chair.

So the wax doll sat all night with its eyes wide open staring ahead like a small dead child. And Dot considered her pigeon-hearted father and wondered why she could never recall his face.

Dot began to eat a little more each day. She dressed, she went downstairs to sit in an armchair. In the evening, Mrs Hollidaye taught her to play Up Jenkins and dominoes and spillikins on a low table by the fire. Loopy Lil hadn't a steady enough hand for spillikins and she couldn't count up to more than three for the dominoes but she seemed happy to watch and smile.

In the morning when the sun was shining through the mist, Dot was wrapped up to go out. She was surprised how bare the gardens had become, except for the lopsided apple tree in the lower orchard whose branches still carried a crop of apples shimmering like tiny brassy moons.

'I like to leave that one unpicked. For the birds, otherwise what will they have to see them through till spring? I call it my bird tree.'

The prisoners of war had left the fields and there were different people who now gathered for elevenses round the kitchen range. There was the man demobbed from his regiment who came to do the garden just as he had before he was called to war. There was the young woman and her baby who had moved into the space above the coach-house, and there was the noisy couple from Luton who had taken over the empty servants' quarters up the back stairs.

'Poor dears, bombed out three times, didn't know which way to turn. But at least they're together now.'

The young woman from the coach-house came in and helped Loopy Lil wash dishes in the scullery while her baby sat on the floor chewing on a bone. The baby was fat and red-faced. It roared if anyone went near it. Dot didn't go near. But she went everywhere else, and wherever she went in house or gardens, the grown-ups smiled and said, 'Good day!', and asked how she was. Nobody told her to be off, or lay off, or push off, or not to touch, or to be careful. I'm getting sound as a roach, Dot told herself.

The gardener found her a length of binding twine in a shed so that she could learn to skip. And the young woman let her tie the grizzling baby into the bath-chair and wheel it around the courtyard to look at the hens.

Dot had lived like this for ever. The days of reading and resting, of sewing and eating and growing, merged one into the next. She didn't miss Gloria. This was where she lived now. It would be like this for ever, no change, the pattern was fixed. She was stronger than a roach, as strong as an ox. No one would ever cut pieces off her while she slept.

Then came the snow and she had to stay in and watch from the window how it piled up against the water butt, how it lay like a blanket along the sills, how it changed the distance from bluey brown to white as far as you could see. Her finger tips turned white as bone, her lips became chapped, and the air was so cold it hurt to breathe. The baby went back to its yelling on the scullery floor.

'My dear! Have you ever seen such a fall as this!' said Mrs Hollidaye as she carried the tea-tray through to the drawing-room. 'I've just measured it with my knitting tape. Six and a half inches! The poor dogs hardly know what to make of it. And the postman says he only just made it through.'

Loopy Lil got stuck in a drift on her way back from the farm with the milk.

'So now, my dears, there's two of you to warm up by the fire!'

Through the snow strode a visitor. He came in at the side door as though he knew his own way.

'You'll find her in the drawing-room,' Dot heard Mrs Hollidaye say. 'Yes, she's simply full of beans now.'

He didn't wear a white jacket like hospital doctors but a heavy greatcoat with the collar turned up and boots dampened with slush. But Dot knew he was a doctor because his hands smelled clean and soapy.

First he sat on the sofa and talked to the dogs. He knew them both by name. Dot took no notice of him. But then he asked her what she was knitting, so she had to answer him, and after that she agreed to let him tap her chest with his rubber hammer, peer into her ears with his pencil light, and press the back of her tongue with one of Mrs Hollidaye's silver apostle teaspoons.

'Say aah!' he said. Then he said, 'Aaha, definitely harvesting time. Ripe and ready for removal, I'd say and not a minute too soon. Miss Dorothy, you've done very well.'

When the doctor had gone, Dot said, 'I got to go back in the hospital, ain't I, Mrs H?'

'Yes, my dear. Dr Trees thinks you're ready.'

'Well you want to know something? I were just pretending to him, because I ain't really full of beans. Truth is, I'm still ever so peaky. And them other doctors said I weren't to go back up London for no operation not till I was A1, else I'd be dead as a herring.'

Mrs Hollidaye seemed not to have heard. She merely suggested there'd be time for a game of spillikins before supper.

After Dot had won two rounds, Mrs Hollidaye said, 'We'll have supper early this evening. You'll need to take a bath tonight, won't you, my dear, so as to be clean as a new pin for tomorrow.'

'Tomorrow! Ain't I going back up London then?'

'No, dear. Dr Trees has most kindly arranged your admission to our local hospital.'

'Oh, no! I ain't going there. Not on your life.'

To have to submit to having a part of one's body removed while one slept was going to be bad. But to have to allow it to be done in a strange place was impossible. Dot knew she couldn't be brave enough for that. 'If I got to have it done, I'll go back to the place I was before, back down the Duke's Ferry Road. Where Baby was and all.'

'You'll find they're very good. Miss Lilian had her teeth done there.'

Mrs Hollidaye steadily poured tea.

'You're booked into what we call the Princess Elizabeth Children's Annexe. We had a silver subscription for the bedspreads and curtains. That's Elizabeth, after our royal princess, you know.'

''Course I know,' said Dot. 'She lives at Buckingham Palace.'

'Then I dare say you also know, my dear, what Princess Elizabeth said during the blitz? How splendidly full of cheerfulness and courage all you young London children are. So that's why they've named the new wing after her. To remind you. For that is exactly how you are going to face tomorrow, aren't you? Full of courage!'

85

It was all so planned. Dot could see no way out. Only a raid could save her now. Or perhaps there was something else? She ran from the room and up to her bedroom where the windows were kept open all day to destroy the germs. It was as cold as an old grave.

Dot stood by the open window. 'God in heaven,' she said, for Mrs Hollidaye had explained how you could speak to the good Lord and sometimes the good Lord spoke back. 'God in heaven, let it snow. And snow and always snow and block up all the paths and roads, fields and ditches.'

15   At the Princess Elizabeth

The snow stayed. It was her friend. Dot woke on that morning that could have been the last morning of her life and knew by the brightness reflected across the ceiling that she was safe, for the roads would still be blocked.

She slid joyfully down from the bed and hopped across the cold carpet to the window. The lawns were as smooth and white as yesterday, and the meadow as white, and all the fields away to the marshes on the faraway horizon. And even beyond would be snowbound, perhaps right as far as the sea.

The snow had made the gardens silent, though not inactive. Mrs Hollidaye had pointed out how one could see creatures even more clearly when they were silhouetted as in a shadow cut-out. A blackbird with its beak gleaming golden against the white, scuttled out from under the rhododendron bushes making a flurry of snow slither off the broad leaves. Then the brownish scurrying of a hare across the top of spiky snow-blown grass. Overhead a seagull circled the treetops, pale feathers shining against the dark grey of a flat sky.

And Dot saw something else alive and moving out there too, brown yet larger than a hare. The huddled figure shambled alongside the yew hedge towards the wicket gate. A curious tramplike person wrapped against the weather in an old shawl. Mrs Hollidaye's shawl. But it was not Mrs Hollidaye.

It was Loopy Lil. What was she doing? Where was she off to before her breakfast?

After Loopy Lil's lurching figure had disappeared, her footprints were left behind in the lawn, not soft white marks like all week, but brownish foot-shaped prints. Plod, plod, spoiling the tidiness.

Downstairs the range was blazing, porridge steaming, eggs coddling.

'Snow's still here!' said Dot cheerfully. 'And I seen two gulls. Black-heads. Long way from home, ain't they?'

'I expect they're hungry,' said Mrs Hollidaye. 'And searching for food, the poor mites. There you are, my dear.'

She placed the porridge bowl in front of Dot with a dollop of honey in the middle and some cream on the edge. Dot watched the honey and cream dissolve and trickle like two rivers to join in a silver and golden spreading lake.

'That's the way, a good breakfast. We'll need it today. Long drive.'

The porridge changed. The honey and the cream disappeared into a mess of grey.

'That snow, it don't look no better,' Dot said. 'Still blinking bad.'

'I believe it *is* relenting, my dear, just an iota and the forecast is certainly more optimistic. We should be fine on the road if we leave plenty of time. I've sent Miss Lilian to do a recce.'

Mrs Hollidaye, supping porridge with her back to the flaming range and her face towards the window exclaimed, 'Why do look, Dorothy! Here's our friend Mister Coal Tit back again. Now I do wonder where he's been.'

The small birds clustered tightly on the swinging coconut were fighting for a firm grip. And beneath their feeding place where yesterday had been snowy white, was today damp and brown with mud and warm droppings.

'Ready for your eggs now, my dear?'

But a distant sickness, a mild headache, had taken Dot's appetite. The pain in her jaw had come back. Or was it in her ear? Or in her throat? She never could locate it. Her spoon dropped listlessly back into the dull porridge lake.

'Never mind, Dorothy. You sit cosily by the range till we're ready. Ah, and here's Miss Lilian back now like the angel of good tidings.'

Loopy Lil blew in through the side door like a bundle of old rags with tiny crystals of white on her woollen hood.

'What's that if it ain't snow?' Dot demanded.

'Sleet. Yes, the weather's definitely taking a turn for the better. Well, don't just stand there, Lilian dear. Come on in. We need that door closed.'

The bearer of bad tidings fumbled with her layers of damp shawls and Dot felt fear on all sides till she was suffocated, as though lying beneath collapsed building rubble. She was trapped. She could do nothing to help herself.

The driveway was still snowed up, but once they reached the road there was a narrow track between high mounds on each side.

Loopy Lil came too. Someone had to wipe the inside of the windscreen clear of condensation and clear the outside of the build-up of brown slush.

The journey began but wouldn't end. Dot pulled the tartan rug up over her face to breathe the smell of dogs. She had to have something to hold on to when she disappeared into the black hospital pit.

Mrs Hollidaye was not her next-of-kin so she wasn't allowed to take Dot further than the main entrance where she handed her briskly over to the care of a nurse.

Dot would have liked to have had a hand to hold. Instead, she clutched tightly to the handle of the suitcase Mrs Hollidaye had lent her and followed the nurse along broad passages to a bright room where a group of children, all with suitcases and well wrapped in outdoor clothing, stood huddled like refugees from a foreign land waiting to be told where to go next.

'Come along, children, we can't stand around like lost dogs all day. We've got work to do! Come now, coats off!'

Two were giggling together and seemed to know each other. Dot envied them. She glanced towards the window to catch a glimpse of Mrs Hollidaye's car but the windows, though clear glass, gave on to an enclosed garden with bare rose bushes poking up like black twigs through the slush.

Dot was shown to her bed where a notice was taped with pink sticking plaster to the end rail. She recognized her name but not the other word.

'What's it say?' she asked the nurse who was smoothing out fresh sheets.

' "Tonsillectomy",' said the nurse. 'It's what you're in for, isn't it?'

Dot looked at the other children's beds. They all had this word. Everybody was here for the same thing to be done to them.

'What time?' Dot asked the nurse.

'There's a clock up there on the wall, can't you see?'

Dot tried again. 'I mean, what time is the time they do it. When they put us to sleep. I got to know.'

'Oh, not today! The docs have all gone off long ago.'

'Tomorrow, then?'

'I dare say. All depends. Can you help tuck in that sheet your side? Thanks. You have to be under observation, all of you, for twelve hours beforehand. Didn't they tell you? Then you have to have twelve hours fasting too.'

Dot didn't know what fasting was.

'Not eating nor drinking anything, not even so much as a crumb. Else you may choke.'

Dot wished someone had told Mrs Hollidaye this before, then she wouldn't have wasted all that food feeding her up.

'They wheel you down in batches, two at a time, throughout ops day. All right?'

How? Dot wondered. In pairs marching side by side, or one behind the other? Who would be paired with who? Would the two who already knew each other be together?

'Don't look so worried. It may never happen!'

'Why wouldn't it?'

'No, I don't mean it like that. I mean it's not as bad as you think. You won't know a thing about it. You'll be Harry flatters, out like a light.'

Dot already knew about hospitals. Everything you feared might happen, did happen, only worse. Now that she was back in one, it felt as though she'd never been outside.

Soon, all twenty children were in their beds, stiff in their laundered nightgowns, without having been offered any supper, nor even as much as a sly sip of water. The hands of the clock on the wall dragged round. Dot had time to worry. What if she died like Baby? She didn't mind about that so long as she got a lovely little grave like Mrs Hollidaye's baby daughter. But she knew that Gloria wouldn't think to give her one. Out of sight, out of mind, is what Gloria would say.

Dot wished she'd been given a bed nearer one of the windows so she could see out, or at least by the door. A great big boy was in the bed by the door. When the lights were turned out he began crying.

'I want my Mummy,' he wailed.

'Don't worry, you'll be seeing her again soon,' said a nurse.

Not if he dies, he won't, Dot thought and felt better to realize that at least she wasn't frightened by that.

Next day, Dot was made to lie on a high hard bed in a glittery room without windows and they pressed a black rubber bowl over her face which smelled like the inside of her gas-mask. But instead of protecting her from attack, this mask forced the gas at her, rushing it up into her face with a sinister hissing. As she began to choke she kicked and struggled for breath before tumbling down into nowhere.

But after that, life began again and it was easy to feel full of courage and cheerfulness. They gave the children white ice-cream and red jelly, and brightly coloured drinks clinking with chunks of ice. They let them slide around on the polished floor and listen to music on the ward radio. There was a cupboard full of toys and a shelf of books.

It wasn't at all like staying in hospital.

16   Marrow Jam for Tea

After Mrs Hollidaye had fetched Dot from the Princess Elizabeth, she told her, 'Your mother telephoned, my dear. She would like you home with her now. Isn't that simply grand?'

'Home?' said Dot.

'I explained it was a bit of a flap to go for the train this afternoon. So we'll pop you on the first one tomorrow.'

Tomorrow was too soon.

'What if I don't want to go?' said Dot.

'Yes, I do know, my dear, it's always difficult, isn't it? Having to do things one doesn't want.'

'I can't go back,' Dot said. '*Please*, Mrs H, I want to be here, stay with you. And the dogs. And Miss Lilian.' She thought, I don't belong there any more.

Mrs Hollidaye said, 'Yes, wouldn't that be splendid?' The conversation was over. She said, 'High time to start a new pot of jam. Let's see what we have left. Come, will you, my dear, and help choose?'

Dot followed Mrs Hollidaye into the larder. How could she be concerned about the choice of jam?

'Mrs Parvis hates me. I heard her say I ain't worth the air I breathe.'

'So which is it to be? Quince, cranberry jelly, mulberry? What a decision.'

'And anyway Gloria don't want me neither.'

Gloria still wanted Baby, the apple of her eye.

'See, she's an usherette now, so she don't have time for me no more.'

'My dear, it's probably hard for you to understand, but your mother is very young. And confused. And she needs you.'

92

While Loopy Lil and Mrs Hollidaye were organizing tea, Dot walked slowly round the gardens, dragging her shoes through crunchy heaps of left-behind snow. Mrs Hollidaye was incapable of understanding how the thought of having to leave tomorrow hung on Dot's shoulders like a heavy woollen cloak of despair.

Leaving, said the rooks cawing, leaving, said the trees, leaving, said the pigeons, to leave, leave, leave, said the hens behind their wire enclosure. It gave her a dull all-over pain more acute than any kind of real pain. In the fading light, she began to see things she'd not noticed before. How the bark of the oaks was not brown but pale gold; how primroses were nestling safely amongst tussocks of bristly dry grass. How the leaves which still clung to the branches of the pear tree were silvered on their undersides.

There was nothing like this back at Mrs Parvis's. Back at Mrs Parvis's was an indoor world. Dot remembered how the bowl of each spoon at Mrs Parvis's was stained a streaky brown, and bent crooked at the shaft, with NAAFI stamped on the handle.

She remembered how the table around which they sat at High Tea, was covered with a sheet of speckled grey lino which had a strange stickiness. When you touched it with the edge of your hand, your skin felt as though it had become attached so that you were in danger of becoming a part of Mrs Parvis's table for ever.

In Mrs Parvis's parlour there were greasy patches on the chairs which she covered with little cloths. Along the narrow landing at Mrs Parvis's were laid pieces of carpet to cover the cracks in the lino. At Mrs Parvis's the metal meat-safe hanging from its nail outside the basement room never contained meat, only sausages and suet, with blue-bottles buzzing round.

How could Mrs Hollidaye consider allowing Dot to return to that unsafe place where the air robbed your cheeks of their roses, where buildings collapsed though the bombs had long since stopped, where there was no glass in half the windows, no water in the taps, where nothing was quite what it seemed to be.

At Mrs Parvis's, things were often pretending to be other things, like Mrs Parvis saying one thing when she meant another, things were hiding other things, like scraps of rug concealing cracks, white glass windows concealing sick children.

'And nobody don't want me there anyhow,' Dot finished out loud.

She would stay, here where things were what they seemed to be, where trees were trees, hens were hens.

She went indoors and sat hunched in her coat and mittens on the sofa by the drawing-room fire.

'I ain't going, Mrs H,' she said. 'A million horses ain't going to drag me back there. And there's *him* too. When *he* turns up, *he* ain't going to want me neither. I don't even know what he looks like.'

'Bread and jam, my dear?' said Mrs Hollidaye as though she still had her cloth-ears on. 'Lilian dear, what about you? It's the new marrow and ginger, Dorothy and I chose it this afternoon. Or there's just a little honey left? But we'll save the fresh comb for Dorothy to take back tomorrow.'

'What if I go and don't never get to come back?' said Dot. 'You'll miss me. Then you'll be sorry.' She sounded like Mrs Parvis, saying one thing yet meaning another.

'Nonsense. Of course you'll come back. Everybody always comes back. It's going to be exciting to see your mother again. You'll be able to tell her all the news.'

What news would interest Gloria? Would she want to know about the flowering of the pink camellia and its glossy leaves, about the goat running away, about the double-yolked egg? She might pretend to listen but she wouldn't hear. The two places were quite separate. News of one didn't transmit to the other.

Mrs Hollidaye spooned some chunks of marrow on to a slice of bread, cut it in half, and put it gently into Dot's hand.

'Eat up, there's a good girl. I know, leaving is always hard.'

94

Dot took the bread and sniffed. 'It hurts. Like real hurt. Much worse than being ill.'

'My dear, that's good. You must hold on to the hurt. It's a sign of growing up.'

'But I don't want it like this. I want it to be like it was before.'

Lying in bed and being looked after and enveloped in love, by day and by night.

'Like I was your little girl. Like the one what died.'

She flung herself crying on to Mrs Hollidaye's lap, knocking Mrs Hollidaye's afternoon hat sideways. Mrs Hollidaye straightened it, but let Dot stay.

'You have to remember, Dorothy, that I am your friend. I am not your mother. Why, I'm old enough to be your grandmother! I cannot keep you here when your mother wants and needs you. However, even when you're faraway, this place will still remain, you'll still see it. That way, you have the benefit of both.'

'How?'

'Wipe your nose first, and then I'll tell you something that happened to me. A long time ago. About leaving a place when I felt torn between two people I loved. You see, unlike you who has lived in so many places and seen so much, I had never lived anywhere except at my parents' home. I knew every corner and I loved that house so much. I loved him so much too. I was so excited to be a young bride going off on tour to Europe. Then to a new home waiting for me. But after the marriage and the party, when it was time, the brougham was already waiting for us at the front door, I couldn't bear to leave. Like you now, I felt that I might never come back. Or, even if I did, that things would be different.'

'Did you cry?'

'Goodness gracious me, no! That would never have done. Why, it would have made everyone else so sad. I had to keep the hurt to myself. But my nurse knew.'

'Your *nurse*? If you were ill, why did they make you go away?'

'Not a sick-nurse. My nursemaid, the servant who looked after me. She helped me dress in my new going-away outfit before I went down to say goodbye to my parents. She must have known about the hurt of leaving, for she said, Don't worry, Miss Charlotte. You'll be taking this whole place with you. Whenever you miss it, you close your eyes and you'll find it right there in front of you. You'll see, Miss Charlotte, she told me, how you can walk into every room, check in every cupboard, count the books in your father's library, just as though you were really there.'

'So what did you do?'

'I straightened my back, and I walked down the stairs to my parents and I said goodbye to them and to the servants lined up on the front steps. I still didn't entirely believe my nursie. She was up at the window looking out. But I found out it was all quite true what she'd said.'

Dot found that she had stopped crying and was sitting upright, eating the slice of bread and marrow jam.

That evening, when Mrs Hollidaye crept into Dot's bedroom to damp down the fire for the night and check that the guard was securely in place, she had filled a trug basket with garden produce.

'For tomorrow, my dear,' she whispered. 'I'll put it here by the chair so we don't forget.'

There was a posy of pale spring flowers wrapped in damp newspaper to keep them fresh, a bag of potatoes tied with bristly twine, six eggs in a carton, carrots unearthed from the sandheap in which they had lain stored against invasion of the wire-worm, and a selection of dessert apples, no mere windfalls but blemish-free bests, each polished to a rosy sheen by Loopy Lil.

'You know, my dear,' Mrs Hollidaye said, sitting on the edge of the bed and taking Dot's hand. 'I've often thought that each person is rather like a different vessel out at sea. Some are little dinghys, others great ocean liners. Or paddle steamers, or cork rafts.'

'You mean, like we're all *boats*?' said Dot, surprised.

'That's it. Or ships. Once out on the big seas of life, we

each have to do the best we can, whether we have sails, or engines, or nothing but a wooden paddle. I daresay your brother was like my daughter, a pretty little flower petal bobbing along. He wasn't meant to keep afloat for ever. While you, Dorothy my dear, started out as a small tub, straight into deep choppy waters, with quite a few holes in the bottom, no rudder, no sails. You were scarcely seaworthy. But somehow you were unsinkable. Then you were towed into harbour. Now you've been patched up, your hull's been scraped, a lick of paint and you're ready to get back into the great sea of life. Well, goodnight, my dear.' She bent and kissed Dot on her forehead.

17   Coming Home

The train rattled through the suburbs, then slid between the brick backs of tall tenement blocks where Dot could look right in the windows at women standing by their kitchen sinks.

Then it rumbled along a bridge, so Dot could see into the friendly clutter of people's back yards, down into bomb-sites to view the mystery of chaos.

They said there was a fuel shortage. But Dot saw plenty of coal heaped up beside the tracks in so many different shades of black. Big shiny chunks, thin pale nuggets, dull velvety dust, huge rocks like slippery ice.

At home in the country, Dot thought, we burn wood, chestnut limbs that spit and hiss in the drawing-room, neat oak logs in the bedrooms that quietly glow through the night.

The train passed a fire station, a brewery, and over the wide murky river.

Gloria was late. But the station felt safer than it used to, though nothing had changed except Dot herself. She saw the same high empty space between the ground and the broken glass roof, she recognized the air which smelled of soot and coal-smoke and was thick as grey soup, and the mottled pigeon-droppings and the grey suits of men, the black hats.

She staggered with the laden trug to where the buffers stood up like huge metal pennies on their sides preventing the train from going any further. London was not on the way to somewhere else. London was the centre to which all tracks, all travellers, all patched-up dinghy boats, were lead.

Dot had been away and now she had come back.

Patiently she waited beside the ticket collector till Gloria came running breathlessly across the station towards her. She had her best shoes on, and a new hat. She had her hair in a new way too, short and brushed upwards. It made her look different, almost like a stranger.

'Hello, duckie, so here we are large as life and twice as handsome. That train must have been in ever so early.' She smiled at the ticket collector. 'Here pet, better let me take some of your things.' She took Dot's carriers and Dot carried the trug basket.

Dot said, 'Mrs Hollidaye gave me the money for a cab.'

'Ooh, just hark at you, speaking all lah-de-dah!' Gloria giggled. 'You gone and got yourself a posh accent, just like Mrs H herself.'

'No, I haven't,' said Dot, wondering if she had. 'Anyway, you've gone and changed yourself too. Your hair's gone yellow.'

'Had it bleached. Does it suit? Incendiary blonde,' said Gloria. 'So how much she give you, then?'

'Five bob.'

'You don't want to go wasting that on a taxi. We can get a number nine easy enough. Split the difference on a cuppa, shall we? Let's pop into the Corner House.'

She lead the way through swirling traffic.

'All right by you, duckie? You'd like a nice sticky bun and some tea, wouldn't you?'

In the spacious tea-rooms, a sparkling light was suspended from the ceiling, a man in a suit played the piano and most customers wore hats even daintier than Gloria's new one. But nobody was encumbered with the bounty of the countryside tied up with old newspaper and garden string. Dot shoved the trug out of sight under their table before the waitress saw.

'I got the afternoon off,' said Gloria. 'So there's no hurry on us to get back quick. Since we're in town, we might as well enjoy ourselves while we got the chance. What d'you say to taking in a picture after?'

A waitress scuttled past carrying a cake-stand stacked

99

with glistening and brightly coloured cakes and pastries.

'Haven't seen the like of that for a while then, have we?' said Gloria. 'Ooh and listen, he's playing the melody from that new film. Ooh, did I cry at the end!'

Mrs Hollidaye was right. Dot did still have the garden with her. The dark shape of the yew silhouetted against the corner of the window was quite clear. She could even see a thrush pecking out a scarlet yew berry, swallowing the scarlet flesh and spitting out the poisonous pip. And she could hear the rooks cawing too. She didn't tell Gloria about it. Gloria was busy tapping her feet in time to the music.

'Just like old times, ain't it, before you was took so poorly,' said Gloria. 'Hey, what's pecking at you, pet, giving that long face? You ain't gone and got yourself worked up into a glum mood, have you now?'

Dot thought how she belonged in the country. Now she had to belong here too.

'No, 'course not,' said Dot. 'I'm glad to be back.'

'Well, that's something anyhow. Though you look as though you could do with something to perk you up. Bit of frolic, that's what you been missing.'

The waitress came to take their order.

'Go on then, duckie,' said Gloria. 'Which one d'you fancy? Don't hold back.'

'Ta,' said Dot. 'I'll have one of them with the pink on top.'

18　The Fathers

Dot was pleased when the Children's Officer called at the basement and said she was strong enough to start school. She remembered things from when she'd been to school before.

But she found it was a different school with different faces. Many of these children had been attending for a long time, so they already knew many things, specially the important things like how to stand in line and what to do when your pen-nib broke.

There were good things at school too, cooked dinners every day and milk if you took your own mug.

Dot didn't have a milk-mug but the teacher lent her one. The dinners came by van in metal tins. The milk came in a can and the teacher shared it out with a ladle. Certain children, whose names were on a list, were called up once a day to be given yellow capsules which had to be swallowed in front of the teacher. Dot was among them. She chewed hers and found it contained cod liver oil.

At first, Gloria took Dot along the road to school but it was often difficult for Gloria to get out of bed in time, so they arrived late.

'Miss don't like me being late,' said Dot. 'She says I got a lot of catching up to do. I think I'll go on me own.'

Gloria, under the blanket, agreed. 'Watch your P's and Q's, then,' she mumbled.

A plumber came and installed a row of six washbasins in the cloakroom with running water, hot and cold at each, though they still had to run across the playground in all weathers to reach the outside lavatories. The bars of new yellow soap and the new white linen roller-towels placed beside the washbasins were marked, LCC. Dot found she could read the letters and was surprised. The desks had these same letters stamped into the metal brackets. So did each sheet of lavatory paper which the teacher gave them if they asked, and the box of wax tapers for lighting the gas mantle.

Dot asked the teacher what LCC meant since it was written on so many things.

'London County Council, dear,' said the teacher. 'That's good. So you have been taught to read?'

Dot said No, she didn't think so. But then she found that she must have been without noticing, for she discovered that there was writing everywhere which she could read without even trying. The coal-hole covers along the pavements had words on them. So did the milk-float. A whole sentence was painted on its side. *Express Dairies, the oldest dairy in London*, it said.

There was a lot to look at, so she took a long time coming back after school, stopping to watch the men mending holes in the roads, to watch the demolition team with their mighty metal ball swinging on its chain from the crane clearing the bomb-site, to watch carpenters erecting wooden hoardings around the cleared sites to keep the people out, to see bill-stickers on ladders pasting huge coloured pictures on to the hoardings. She could read them all, *Oxo*, *Rinso*, *O-Cedar*, and *Aero*, even if she didn't always understand what they meant. Then she dawdled through the mews where the milk-horses were shod, and the blacksmith made new railings to put in front of the houses.

But she had given up telling Gloria about what went on each day. Gloria wasn't interested.

'I got things on me mind just now, ducks,' she said. 'Can't you see?'

She was always rushing off to the Housing Applicant Office and the interviews took a long time.

'There's a lot of other people after the same thing,' Gloria explained.

Then one afternoon she came in smiling.

'They're giving us the extra points! Because of your health, pet, they're putting us on the priority list, say we didn't ought to be below-ground, nor too high. Ground floor, they say on account of your chest. They're going to start building lots of new flats. Over the river, near the stray dogs' home. They say we might get to have one. Two bedrooms, indoor toilets, hot and cold running to kitchen, so you'll be able to wash your hands whenever you want.'

Dot didn't tell her that at school they already had hot and cold water and she could wash her hands and face at any time.

'Sixteen and sixpence a week. Mind you, I don't know where we'll find that.' The rent to Mrs Parvis was only ten shillings. 'But once your father comes home, things'll start perking up, won't they?'

But being on a priority list didn't, after all, seem to make any difference. They went on waiting.

'Fat lot of use that office is. All hot air and not much more,' said Gloria. 'There's hundreds of us on priority. They ain't got nothing for us. D'you know, me and your Dad, we had a lovely home out at the start. A beautiful room, all our own. Pink curtains we had there and ever such a nice tea service. Then there I was come back from ante-natal and it was blown clean away. Funny how you forget things when you ain't got them no more.'

Dot thought, I've forgotten his face. But I haven't forgotten he's coming back.

At the school, there were two other girls whose fathers had not yet returned. Then, in the playground, one of them whispered, 'Mine ain't coming back. Ever. My Nan told me last night.'

Dot envied her. Viv didn't seem upset about it either. She just shrugged. 'He died or something, I don't know.'

Then a few days later, the other girl, Sally, came dancing across the playground and said she'd just got hers back.

'He was in a camp. He's a bit thin, though.'

'Where he been?' Dot asked. She had seen pictures in the newspaper that Mrs Parvis had delivered every day of men and women who'd been kept locked up in a camp till the Americans came and found them. They were thin. Had Sally's father been in one of those places too, in striped pyjamas with shaven head?

'No, not him. Them's the Jews you're thinking of. Mine was in Burma,' said Sally.

'That's ever such a long way off,' said Dot. 'I expect.'

'Yeah, it was hot over there and he didn't have nothing to eat except rats. That's what he says. I dunno if he's making it up. You can't eat rats. D'you want to come and have a look at him?'

She was so proud of this father. She talked about him all day. Then she invited Dot and three others to walk home with her after school. She lived in a big old tenement block. They climbed up to the top floor and stood around in the corridor while Sally went in to fetch him out.

'Here he is!' she said at last. 'My Daddy!'

A thing appeared in the doorway beside her. It looked to Dot more like a skeleton in clothes than a father. He had heavy army trousers held up with a huge leather belt and a thick army shirt. Inside the clothes there was nothing. Brown sticks stuck out of the sleeves where there should have been wrists and his head was like a hard dry acorn, sun-burned and bald, no hair. The children backed away. They didn't know what to do. Then the mouth opened and the father's skull smiled. That was the worst bit.

The other three turned and bolted off down the stairs. Dot stayed just long enough to smile back. He was so thin he looked like even the birds wouldn't want to peck at him. He looked as though he'd crack if you touched him.

'See you tomorrow,' she called to Sally but couldn't think of anything to say to the man, so she ran off after the others.

Next morning, Dot was surprised when Gloria got up early and left for the Housing Applicant Office the same time as she went to school.

'They're running a draw for the houses,' Gloria explained.

'A draw?' said Dot.

'A lucky dip like. They ain't got enough homes. They

want to make it fair. We're each going to get a ticket. I just know it's me lucky day.'

In the evening Gloria cried a bit when she came home. Dot comforted her. She had waited all day in a hall with her lottery number. But it hadn't been her lucky day after all. Her name wasn't picked from the hat.

'All I wanted was to get moved in somewhere nice before he comes back.' Dot wanted to tell her how they were much better staying just as they were. No home. No father.

Gloria had missed High Tea. Wearily she took off her stockings and hung them on the back of the chair to get ready for bed. She inspected her bare feet and started to paint the toe-nails. Dot watched as her mother applied the shiny flame-red lacquer to each toe-nail.

'You're getting yourself ready for him coming back, ain't you?' Dot said.

She had decided what must have happened to him, why he was taking so long to return, and why she could never recall his face.

'He were a pilot, weren't he?' she said. A fuel tank had exploded. He had caught alight. 'Got his face all burned up. Like them men we saw on the newsreel, ain't he?'

Gloria snapped back, 'No, I told you before, he weren't never a pilot. Never went up in the air. Though don't you go thinking, just because a fellow don't get airborne, didn't stop me liking him. In my own way.' And she went back to her painting.

Dot stroked her mother's other white leg stretched out along the bed, with the varnish drying on the toes now like five scarlet flames.

'You got ever such nice legs,' Dot said. 'Hope I get legs like yours when I grow up.'

'Oh, leave me alone with your silly talk, can't you!' said Gloria, then softened and gave Dot's cheek a gentle pinch. 'Your Dad once said how I had legs like Betty Grable. So you'll have to put on a bit more flesh if you want filmstar legs. Still, you're coming along, aren't you now?'

Dot wanted to know, if he wasn't a pilot, what did he do?

'He were a rigger, supposed to be.'

Dot didn't know what a rigger was.

'Important job. Planes can't take off without the rigger there to pull away the chocks. Maybe he'll tell you about it himself some time.'

Dot hoped not.

19 The Dancer in the Street

Next day there was music outside school. After the register, the evening prayer, the curtsies and bows to teachers, and the let-out bell, Dot ran with the others across the playground, through the iron gate, towards the jangling sounds.

Clustered on the narrow pavement were the waiting mothers with outstretched hands, the mothers with prams, the mothers with toddlers attached to their skirts.

Children surged forward to find the music. Some mothers held their children tightly, letting them watch from a safe distance but not too close.

The dancing man was standing out in the middle of the road as though unaware of the scarlet double-decker which might trundle down the High Street at any moment to knock him down. He had a monkey and a performing cat. The monkey in a waistcoat was on a chain attached to the dancing man's belt. The cat wore a jewelled collar. He didn't seem to see the crowd of mothers and children watching him. He ignored everything except his music-making, his monkey, and his cat.

He was a misshapen giant, hunch-backed by the drum attached to his shoulders which seemed to beat by itself. His knees were distorted by brass cymbals attached on the inner leg. Brass bells hung like bunches of ripe grapes to each thigh. He played first a whistle, then a mouth organ, then a trumpet.

He seemed to have a score of hands and a hundred musical fingers. His toes danced, his elbows danced. His monkey skipped and pulled on its lead and held out a tin cup to the crowd.

He was the most beautiful creature Dot had ever seen, a creation of this city which was the centre of the world. You'd never in a million years see a dancing man in a field in the country. Yet when he trilled on the water-whistle, he seemed to create birds singing in the branches of invisible trees overhead.

'Well, fancy that!' said one of the mothers. 'Haven't seen a one-man band since way back. Times must be getting better.'

'It's cruel,' said another.

Dot thought at first she meant it was unkind for the man to be so constricted by the many instruments strapped to all parts of his body. But she must have meant the monkey, for another mother said:

'It's only an animal. It doesn't mind. My brother saw monkeys when he was coming back through Gibraltar. They were quite tame he said. Look, it's smiling. And I once saw a dancing bear when I was little. It liked it, you could tell. It really liked dancing.'

Some of the mothers let their children dart forward to drop a penny in the monkey's mug, though none let their children too close. Dot had no meeting mother to restrain her. She was free to go as close to the man's music as she dared, to stare as long as she wanted, to dance on the kerb right beside him where he seemed so tall he almost blacked out the sky, and the music so overwhelming you could hear nothing else.

The others drifted away. Dot stayed. She longed to ask what was his monkey's name, though she knew she mustn't speak to strangers. So, when still playing, still marking time with the great drum strapped to his back and clashing the cymbals, still rattling the bells, and making the melody with his mouth organ, he began to half-dance, half-walk down the middle of the road, she followed a few paces behind and safely on the pavement. He never looked round. He never asked for money. Where would he go next?

Nobody stopped her following. Perhaps they thought she was part of his troupe?

Where was he going? Where were they now? His music so changed the streets that the gas lamps looked brighter, the spiked railings more friendly, the painted front doors more brightly coloured than where she lived. Then she saw how the Oxo boy on the advertisement hoarding smiled and she realized that they had come a different way by a different route and that she was nearly at Mrs Parvis's boarding house.

The dancing man stopped playing and as he turned to unbuckle the strap of his cymbals, he saw Dot was still behind him.

'You'd best go home now, lassie,' he said. 'Back to your Mum and Dad before they start to miss you.'

Dot wanted to tell him that she hadn't got a dad. But she knew that telling things the way you wanted them to be rather than the way they were didn't change anything for longer than the moment of the lie. She said, 'My Dad's not home from the war yet.'

'He will be. So you better be ready for him,' said the dancing man. Then he picked up his monkey and the cat and strode away with the bells on his knees jangling.

20   The Man who Went to War

Dot was glad she'd been warned by the dancing man because there was no warning from Gloria. In the morning Dot went off to school and he wasn't there. In the afternoon, she came home and he was.

Mrs Parvis was standing out on the front doorstep, pretending to watch out for something in the sky. Dot knew what she was really up to, waiting to be first with bad news. She didn't like it when Dot slipped in unseen and with Mr Brown gone off to college, she hadn't so many people who would listen to her.

'He's back, then,' she said.

'What?' said Dot.

'Not "what". "Who".'

Dot's heart began pounding, first with ᴀ .xiety, then with an irrational hope that it just might be Mr Brown who was back.

'Downstairs. Your Ma went to pick him up this morning.'

Dot tried to edge by.

'So he'll be popping up to the palace with the rest of them, to pick up his medals.' But she said it as though she already knew different, for then, as though speaking to another invisible adult, she added, 'I *don't* think. If there's one thing I've learned out of the past six years, it's that anybody can get out of anything if they try hard enough.'

Dot managed to wriggle past and down the stairs, and there in the basement room sat the man in the drab, ill-fitting, demob suit.

He wasn't a smiling skullman, he wasn't a melted airman. He had a blank sort of face, and that was about all there was to him. No twinkling sky-blue eyes to match a

110

sky-blue uniform. No bright rainbow of medal ribbons on his breast.

Dot knew from just looking at him that he was no hero, no villain either. He wasn't anything much. He was a nothing.

She felt almost relieved. Maybe she'd known it all along. There was that thing Mrs Hollidaye said, about how each person could only be brave in their own way and there wasn't room on earth for everybody to be a hero. She'd told Dot there'd got to be the ordinary people too so that the few could be visibly valiant. He was one of the ordinary ones.

Dot sat herself cross-legged on the bed and watched him perched on the chair by the window, blinking and twitching and fidgeting but never looking her way, then seeming to fall asleep and looking quite young, younger than Mr Brown anyhow, and certainly not at all like Sally's dad who'd been to Burma and eaten rats.

Gloria was next door making a pot of tea in Mrs Parvis's kitchen. When she came in carrying the tin tea-tray with a scratched picture of Buckingham Palace, she whispered, 'Don't stare like that. It's not nice. Haven't you no manners?'

'Just trying to get used to him, ain't I? He don't look too well, do he?' People used always to be saying that about her. Now she could say it about someone else.

Slowly, he took off the jacket and folded it neatly into a rectangle which he placed on his knee. Gloria took it from him to hang on the back of the door. He sat down again on the very edge of the chair and they drank the tea in silence. He moved slowly, like a tired man wading through cold water. He didn't look at Dot. He didn't look at Gloria either.

'We don't have much sugar left,' said Gloria. 'D'you take sugar?' Then, 'Mrs Parvis says she'd be obliged to have your ration book as soon as possible if you please.'

Dot wanted to ask, He hasn't got a wooden leg has he? But she knew he hadn't. Some of those boisterous brave men with stretched paper faces, with stumpy two-pincered hands, and tiny lidless eyes, had lost legs as well. This one had both legs and all his fingers, yet you still felt there was something missing.

'And you better start calling me Mum,' said Gloria. 'It'd be more natural like, now we're a family.'

It didn't feel natural.

'And you call him Dad.'

Dot wasn't going to call him anything.

That night, Dot was to sleep on two extra blankets folded over to make a thin mattress for he, the man, would be in the bed where Dot used to sleep.

It was not uncomfortable down on the floor, just lonely. Dot used to have Gloria to snuggle up to in the dark. Not any more. Gloria had to belong with him now.

She tried not to wish he could go away even though the room was cramping them.

After school, she took as long as she could dawdling back. He was still there lying down with his eyes shut. Dot guessed he might have been only pretending. Dot wondered if they'd been arguing. She beckoned Gloria into the dark passage outside the room.

'You got to tell me,' she whispered. 'Where's he *been*? Why's he *like* that?'

'Who's "He"? The cat's father? I can't hear if you don't talk proper,' said Gloria in a low voice. 'Speak nice and call him Dad.'

'But what's *wrong* with him?'

'Oh heck, ducks, you might as well know. He was a nutter. Went barmy in the army you might say!' She laughed, but it wasn't a real laugh. 'That place I took you, run by the military, that was like a sort of special asylum.'

Dot didn't know what an asylum was. She thought it was a kind of prison. So had he done something wrong?

'Nervous collapse they called it. He was a mental, couldn't even speak a threepenny bit.'

Dot thought of Loopy Lil. She was a mental. She was also a safe and kind person to be with. If her father got like that, then it might be all right.

112

'Loopy Lil's different,' said Gloria. 'She were born that way. Your old man started out OK. When he got called up he was good as the best of them. First time I see him in his uniform, he looked that lovely I could've eaten him alive. It was thinking too much, about the fighting, what did for him, got him all confused. It was a kind of illness, in the head.'

Dot remembered what it was like when she had felt so ill and confused.

'He didn't like none of it, so he sort of copped out, gave up eating one fine day, till he couldn't stand up no more, couldn't do what he was told on the airfield. Last war, men who did what he done, they called them deserters. Used to take them out and shoot them in the head. That cured their problems darn quick.'

'I'm glad they don't do that no more,' Dot said. She wondered, did Gloria still love him?

'What kind of funny question is that?'

'Was it like when I was ill and couldn't eat? Maybe he needs to get a breath of fresh air. Maybe you should take him down to Mrs Hollidaye's. Get some roses in his cheeks. I got better, didn't I?'

'Can't do that, ducks. He's been discharged. He ought to start looking for work now.'

He wasn't really sleeping. He heard them whispering by the door. He rolled over and opened his eyes though he didn't look at Dot any more than she looked at him. He looked over at Gloria.

'It's her what should go away and stay,' he said. 'It's not right her having to be cooped up in here with me. She don't like me. She's scared.'

'Am not!' Dot wanted to explain it was more that she just didn't know him yet, and she was sorry about him being ill.

'That woman who's been good to you, would she have her if you asked?'

Gloria nodded.

He took a ten shilling note from his trouser pocket and gave it to Gloria.

'She'd be all right on the train?'

'Oh, yes,' said Gloria. 'She's a sensible kid, aren't you, duckie? And she likes it down there.'

He took four pennies from his other pocket.

'She know how to use the phone?' he asked.

''Course I do,' Dot said.

'She got the lady's number?'

'Yes.'

Gloria said, 'All right then, love. You do as your Dad says. Hop on over to the end of the road and give her a tinkle. Ask if you can come down for a day or two. I can tell school you been took poorly again.'

Dot walked down the road slowly to give herself time to think what to say. She wanted so much to go to Mrs Hollidaye's, for a long time. Yet she sensed that it might be like telling things the way you wanted them to be rather than the way they really were. It would be like running away from him back at the basement. Dot decided she wouldn't invite herself to stay but would wait till Mrs Hollidaye asked her.

She dialled the number carefully and heard the distant ringing tone. She could imagine it clanging across the hall, up the stairway, along the draughty corridors, around the drawing-room and out through the open windows. She wanted to go and yet didn't want to go both at once.

She heard Mrs Hollidaye's voice answer and she pressed Button A to let the pennies clatter through and they were connected.

'Hello, there, Mrs H. It's me, Dorothy here. How's yourself, then?'

Mrs Hollidaye sounded pleased. She asked Dot about whether the sun was shining in London, about the school, and about Gloria.

Dot said they were all A1 and tip-top.

Then Mrs Hollidaye told Dot about Loopy Lil, about the dogs and the hens, and about her son whose ship was due home from the Pacific any day now.

Dot kept expecting Mrs Hollidaye to ask her to come down and stay. Why didn't she?

Dot said, 'We didn't get the flat we was after. So Gloria's put in for one of them new pre-fabs.'

Mrs Hollidaye said she had read about them. 'Pre-fabricated temporary emergency housing. How perfectly champion.'

'If we get one, we'll have two bedrooms, so I'll have me own window to look out of. I've always wanted me own window. But they don't build them,' Dot explained. 'The walls come on this lorry, all ready made, in pieces with the windows stuck in. Ours ain't arrived yet.'

Still Mrs Hollidaye didn't mention Dot going to stay. So Dot said, 'And Derek's back too.'

'Your father? Why this is excellent news too, my dear.'

'But he don't look too hot. It's because he's been ill like, in the head.'

'Another casualty of the conflict. But he'll win through.'

'I feel like he's the child, and I've got to be the adult.'

'I know you and your mother will be doing your very best for him. A loving family is the best medicine till he's on his feet again.'

'I'm going to buy him some flower seeds,' said Dot. 'For him to plant. See, when we get the pre-fab, we get this little titchy bit of space round the edge, so I was thinking of us having a garden.'

'Why, that really is simply splendid news, my dear. Nasturtiums would be good if you want something quick. Or sweet peas. They don't take up much space. You must let me know as soon as you know when you're moving, won't you? And we've quite a few bits and bobs of furnishing that your mother might find useful. And of course I'll send you up some cuttings. How exciting. I do like to hear about a new garden in the planning. Hostas do well, in sun or shade, spring bulbs of course, maybe a few montbretia? Any soil, and they multiply so easily. Gardening's a wonderful medicine too.'

Dot started to say, 'I hope I can bring my Dad down to visit you some day.' But the money ran out, so she was cut-off in mid-sentence. She wasn't sure if Mrs Hollidaye had heard. She hoped she hadn't heard any of it. Like the dancing man said, she had to get back to her Mum and Dad. They had to stick together and be a family.

Dot unrolled her piece of twine and began to skip slowly along the pavement over the coal-hole covers towards the basement. She was glad she wasn't going away again just now. This was the world where she belonged.

'We have to live where we live,' Dot said out loud to the dusty street. Then she began to think to herself about which would be best, nasturtiums or sweet peas.

The Doll's House

ISBN 0 19 271734 0

'Oh, wicked,' she sighed. It was a miniature house. She felt sure she'd seen it before. Then she realized it was one of those dream houses from inside her mind.

Becks, a rebellious young girl who won't go to school but dreams of her 'perfect house'; Patrick, a very ill teenager who has to stay in bed; Miss Amy Winters, an elderly spinster who looks back on her past and on a very special birthday present. Three very different people with something in common – the doll's house.

And then there are the dolls, who watch and wait but can never intervene.

'An original novel which explores a number of quite difficult areas ... I enjoyed it very much.' *The School Librarian*

Black Water
ISBN 0 19 271728 6

Albert Edward suffers from what was called the falling sickness, and is now known as epilepsy. Because of this, he is locked away, believed by some to be mad and not worth educating. *Black Water* is the story of how he discovers the truth about his shameful secret, learns to live with it, and finds a way forward into the world with the encouragement of an eccentric old painter called Edward Lear. Lear himself had epilepsy, and the book draws on his own diaries to provide authentic detail.

'A rewarding and enriching reading experience for 12 to 14 year olds; it would be difficult to praise this book too highly.'
The School Librarian

'The characters live off the page. They touch us, we believe in them and in their story . . . It is splendidly written.'
The Guardian